Becca shivered and drew her coat closer around her.

In the distance, a shimmering horizon floated between the ominous afternoon clouds and the flat, foreboding plain.

A chill wind whistled through its slatted sides and around the corners of the old train station, whipping up dirty drifts of snow.

The wheels of the departing train ground faster, spewing out hot sparks that glittered and fell dead on the gray wooden planks at her feet. Through the ephemeral swirl of smoke, she saw Peter standing at the far end of the platform, his legs apart, his hands thrust into the pockets of his jeans. The collar of his jacket was pulled up to his ears and his Stetson pulled low over his eyes.

Slowly, hesitantly, she moved toward him. She wondered how he would greet her. Not the way she had imagined. She held no hope for that.

But when she had almost reached him, he opened his arms and she walked into them, and he held her, close and warm— and she could almost believe things might be as they should.

RACHEL DRUTEN is a native Californian. She is an artist as well as an author, wife, mother, and grandmother. Much of her time is devoted to overseeing a nonprofit, onsite, after-school program in the arts for disadvantaged children kindergarten through grade 5.

Books by Rachel Druten

HEARTSONG PRESENTS
HP312—Out of the Darkness (with Dianna Crawford)
HP363—Rebellious Heart
HP508—Dark Side of the Sun
HP551—Healing Heart
HP627—He Loves Me, He Loves Me Not
HP651—Against the Tide

The Long Road Home

Rachel Druten

Heartsong Presents

This book is dedicated to our son Chad, the "rock" of our family,
and our daughter, Noel, always an inspiration for my heroines.

I am blessed with a quadrumvirate of editors, more than that, dear
friends: Dianna Crawford, Sheila Herron, and Barbara Wilder, and
my husband, Charles, who exercises patience and understanding as
well as his red pencil.

Especially, I want to thank Rev. Dr. Roger O. Douglas, interim
rector, St. Margaret's Episcopal Church, Palm Desert, California,
whose sermon on death was the inspiration for the end of chapter 6.
Much of the dialogue was verbatim from that sermon.

A note from the Author:
*I love to hear from my readers! You may correspond with
me by writing:*

Rachel Druten
Author Relations
PO Box 721
Uhrichsville, OH 44683

ISBN 978-1-60260-059-1

THE LONG ROAD HOME

All scripture quotations are taken from the King James Version of the
Bible.

All of the characters and events in this book are fictitious. Any resem-
blance to actual persons, living or dead, or to actual events is purely
coincidental.

*Our mission is to publish and distribute inspirational products offering
exceptional value and biblical encouragement to the masses.*

PRINTED IN THE U.S.A.

author's notes

More than 200,000 children, orphaned, abandoned, or from families unable to care for them, rode "orphan trains" between 1854 and 1930. Most of the children came from big cities in the East and were sent west to farming communities. The intention was good but not always successful. Some found happy homes, but many were exploited or mistreated; others were separated from their siblings. *Orphan Train Rider: One Boy's True Story* by Andrea Warren and *Orphan Trains: The Story of Charles Loring Brace and the Children He Saved and Failed* by Stephen O'Connor are excellent resources in which to learn more.

Into the twentieth century in medical schools throughout the United States, female students were scorned, discriminated against, and humiliated beyond what I felt comfortable describing in this book.

The first medical school was established in 1767, but it wasn't until 1847 that Elizabeth Blackwell was told she might attend medical school—if disguised as a man. Between 1848 and 1895 seventeen women's medical schools were founded, all staffed by men, since no women doctors were available. Male physicians feared the "feminization" of medicine would lead to a second-class profession.

As late as 1906, Dr. Claudia Potter of Texas was hired at the Temple Sanitarium, not only to work as an anesthesiologist but as a pathologist, house doctor, stretcher boy, and "general flunky" for the paltry sum of $25 a month plus room and board. Hers was not an isolated experience.

In addition to my Internet research, I found Cathy Luchetti's book *Medicine Women: The Story of Early-American Women Doctors* rich with anecdotes and information.

And finally, Whispering Bluff, Colorado, exists only in my mind and heart, as I hope it will in yours.

one

October 1891

Trepidation and resentment filled the heart of ten-year-old Rebecca Hostettler. From the window seat in her upstairs bedroom, she stared past the red barn and across the open wheatland and the dusty road dissecting it. In the distance, she could see the schoolhouse, tiny and white against the flat, dry plain. Farther, barely visible over the horizon, sprang the spire of Whispering Bluff Good Shepherd Community Church: the source of her foreboding.

In the distance, a dark speck appeared on the road. Becca watched it grow larger until she recognized Pastor David's black buggy—until she could see he was not alone.

Three hours ago, she had been sitting right where she was now, when her reverie was interrupted by the telephone ringing in the entry hall below. Two short rings and a long one. A call for their house. She'd raced down the stairs, slid across the polished wood floor, and was just about to reach for it when her father strode out of his library across from the parlor. "I've got it," he said, unhooking the receiver from the box.

Becca shrugged and strolled past him with an air of nonchalance, heading toward the front veranda as if they received telephone calls every day. Then, when her father wasn't looking, she took a quick step right and into the parlor where she slipped behind the half-open door. It was against house rules for her to eavesdrop, but they were on a party line and the operator, Hazel Pryce, spread gossip like a hummingbird spreads pollen. If Becca didn't eavesdrop, everyone in the town of Whispering Bluff would know her family business before she did.

"Hello, David," her father said.

Pastor David Bartlett was her father's best friend. Her father was head deacon at the church, and Becca was convinced he and her mother paid way too much attention to the minister's opinion.

"Was there a good turnout yesterday?"

Her father was talking about the folks who had gathered at Good Shepherd Community Church to look over the children from the orphan train. It was the biggest event in Whispering Bluff, Colorado, since two years ago when President Benjamin Harrison made a brief stop on the Fourth of July. Signs had been posted all over town and flyers distributed. One was still on her father's desk.

CHILDREN
WITHOUT HOMES
FRIENDS FROM THE COUNTRY PLEASE
COME AND SEE THEM

ALL EXPENSES OF TRANSPORTATION ARE PAID BY
THE CHILDREN'S AID SOCIETY
R. TROTTER, AGENT
24 ST. MARKS PLACE, NEW YORK

Pastor David had been active in promoting the placement of orphans in suitable families.

"There was a time," her father was saying, "that Faith and I might have considered adopting one of them ourselves, a companion for Becca."

Glad it didn't get beyond the considering stage, Becca thought. *I have plenty of companions: you, Mama. . .my horse. . . .*

She loved her life. She loved that she was an only child and had all of her parents' attention. She loved that she didn't have to share them with anybody.

Whenever her mama got a baby inside her, Becca used to get excited at the possibility of having a little brother or sister.

But when Mama would lose the baby, and she always did, Becca remembered her parents' sadness that Becca thought would never go away. Her mama would cry, even as she held Becca close.

And then one day, her daddy took her up on his knee. She remembered how he wrapped his arms around her and kissed her on the cheek. "You're enough for us, Becca." And that's the way it had been ever since.

Becca put her eye to the crack in the door and saw her father leaning against the wood-paneled wall.

"Faith and I were sorry not to be there to help, but she was having one of her spells. She has her good days and her bad. You know how it goes. Were all the children chosen?"

Her father paused for the answer. "One wasn't? Poor lad. So where is he now?" Absently he scratched his nose, listening. "You and Sarah can't keep him, not with those four little girls and another on the way." Then he laughed. "Now I understand. So this wasn't just a friendly call. All right, David. We might be able to take him, but only temporarily."

Take him? A total stranger? And an orphan at that!

Her father was silent, still listening. "As soon as Faith and I discuss it, I'll get back to you."

Her father replaced the receiver and started down the back hall to the kitchen. Over his shoulder he called, "I know you're there, Becca!"

The kitchen was the hub of their home, a large and happy place where Becca helped her mother prepare their food, where they prayed over their meals at the large trestle table in the middle of the room, and where they played games. Where, in the evenings, they gathered in front of the stone fireplace: Mama in the rocker, sewing; Papa in his comfortable chair, reading aloud from the Bible or the *Farmers' Almanac*; Becca curled up at his feet; and Max, the dog, curled up at hers.

It was also the place for family conferences. Becca followed her father into the room.

It was a lazy Saturday afternoon. The chores were done,

the lunch dishes put away. A small fire flickered on the fireplace grate, adding cozy warmth to the tableau of her mother in the rocker, stitching ribbon onto the collar of a new dress Becca would wear to church tomorrow. The fabric was lavender wool with a gathered skirt and pink ribbon trim.

Becca preferred coveralls.

Sometimes it made her crazy the way her mother tried to turn her into a "Miss Prissy" with dresses sewn from a Butterick pattern, all gathers and frills, just like the picture on the envelope. To make matters worse, cabbage roses papered her bedroom walls and lace curtains hung at the window.

Her mother looked up over her pince-nez, the small, round glasses balanced on the bridge of her nose. "Who rang us, Jacob?"

"David," he said, taking a seat at the table.

"Oh? What was on his mind?"

"He has a boy from the orphan train who he's trying to find a place for. Thought of us."

"Surprise, surprise." Becca glared at her father as she sat down across from him.

"Don't be sarcastic, missy." Her mother cast her a warning glance. "How old is the lad, Jacob?"

"He's Becca's age. Ten."

"My age?"

Her father nodded. "David said he thought of us right off. A good Christian family, help for me out here on the farm. . .a companion for Becca."

Becca lunged up from the table. "I hope you remember that you told Pastor David if you took him it was only temporary."

"Listening in on conversations again, Becca?" Even though it was phrased as a question, her mother's tone implied it was not.

Becca sat down abruptly, averting her gaze.

"Becca's right. I said if we took him it would be only until David could find him a good home. With your health the way it is—"

"Piffle my health. If I can deal with this obstreperous young 'un"—she cast her daughter a look of amused tolerance—"I can deal with anyone."

"Boys are not as easy," Becca muttered.

"I doubt that," her mother murmured, making a number of careful stitches on the ribboned collar. She laid the dress aside and dropped the glasses from her nose, letting them dangle from a chain pinned to her blouse. Shaking her head, she looked up at her husband. "I know those folks have the best intentions. But sometimes I wonder if the poor little urchins are that much better off. Gathered up and put on orphan trains and sent all over the country for folks to pick over and choose, like. . .like cattle at the county fair."

"A lot of those children are saved from the streets and find good homes," her husband reminded her.

"Sometimes. But a lot of them are exploited." Becca's mother's eyes flashed. "Carl Fischer and his wife have had three different boys in the last two years, and every one of them has run away."

"Carl claimed it was just bad luck." Even Becca's father sounded dubious.

"My foot! You know as well as I do that all Carl and Maude wanted was a free slave."

Becca piped up. "I sure never seen any of them at school."

"Saw. *Saw* them at school," her mother corrected.

"At least the boys were fed and clothed," her father said, "which is probably better than they were used to."

"Then why did they run away?" His wife sniffed. "Besides, children need more than clothes and food. They need nourishment for their hearts and minds and souls." Her mother's cheeks were pink. "They need to be loved and to learn the ways of the Lord. That's what children need. . . . Short supply in Carl's home, I reckon."

Sighing, she adjusted her pince-nez on her nose again and picked up her sewing. "It's unfortunate that there aren't more kindly people like David to look out for the poor little dears."

She shook her head sadly.

Becca was beginning to sense the direction in which her softhearted parents were going, and she didn't like it one bit. If some orphan boy were to get a foothold in her family, there was no telling what would happen.

"And to be the only one not chosen." Her papa wagged his head.

"There's gotta be a good reason," Becca blurted.

Her mother pointedly ignored her. "Can you imagine. . . ? All the other children chosen and you standing alone. It's enough to break your heart." She shook her head then suddenly perked up. "You know," she said thoughtfully, "I think God had a hand in this."

Oh no, here it comes.

"I say He wouldn't have brought the lad here if He didn't expect us to take him."

"Sight unseen?" Her father gave his wife a crooked smile.

Becca couldn't contain herself any longer and jumped to her feet again. "Don't I get any say in this?"

Very deliberately her mother put down her sewing, removed her spectacles, and folded her hands in her lap.

When her face assumed that righteous expression, Becca knew very well what was coming next.

" 'And the King shall answer and say unto them, Verily I say unto you, inasmuch as ye have done it unto one of the least of these my brethren, ye have done it unto me.' "

Becca clenched her teeth but just couldn't help it—she rolled her eyes.

"That's it, young lady!" Her father grabbed her arm. She could get away with almost anything with her father *except* when she was disrespectful to her mother. "You will go to your room and remain there until further notice."

"And," her mother added, "you may make good use of your time by copying Matthew 25, verse 40, thirty times in your best handwriting. By that time, you should have it memorized."

"But, Daddy, you said the boy would stay only a little while, temporarily."

"And what has that to do with your eye-rolling rudeness?"

And that's how Becca happened to be in her room on that late October afternoon, staring out the window—after having completed thirty copies of Matthew 25, verse 40—when Pastor David's black buggy rolled up the dirt drive and parked beneath the old oak that shaded the front veranda.

two

"Becca, you may come out of your room now." Her six-foot-two-inch father filled the doorway, his hand resting against the frame. "There's someone downstairs I want you to meet."

Her mother would have given her a lecture on how to behave. Her father figured she knew and just gave her an encouraging smile.

Becca loved her mother dearly, but the woman was prone to preach. She was the spiritual backbone of the family and Becca's conscience. And she insisted on teaching not only manners and womanly virtues but the womanly arts of tatting, needlepoint, and serving tea—to a less than enthusiastic Becca.

Becca was her father's girl. Tall, like him—the tallest girl in her class. She had his auburn hair and gray eyes, his love of books and growing things and animals. In fact, she already had decided that she was going to college to become a veterinarian. Then she'd come back to Whispering Bluff and live in this house with Mama and Papa forever.

Indeed, she had memorized Matthew 25, verse 40, that afternoon. How could she not, after copying it thirty arduous times in her best handwriting? She really should be repentant after that. But with no face to put with the deed, it was still hard for her to imagine "doing unto" anyone who was going to usurp her parents' attention and disrupt her happy life.

As she followed her father from her bedroom, she could smell the pot roast cooking.

Wouldn't you know they'd show up at dinnertime?

Her pace slowed. Her father had already reached the bottom step when Becca put a reluctant foot on the midfloor landing. Below, her mother stood by the parlor door, looking up with a smile on her lips and a warning in her eyes. Pastor David, shiny black boots planted firmly in the middle of the entry hall, stood robust and sturdy in a solemn black suit befitting his station, his clerical collar, as always, slightly askew. Turning the brim of his stovepipe hat between his fingers, he smiled up at her. "God bless you, Becca, pretty as ever."

Beside him stood a puny kid with a scrawny neck and legs as thin as twigs. His hand-me-down knickers hung loose around his calves, and the rolled-up sleeves of his tweed jacket came halfway down over his knuckles.

He was the sorriest-looking ten-year-old Becca had ever seen. Not at all like the sturdy farm boys she was used to. And short. Why, he was so short he looked no bigger than Eric Straghorn, and Eric was only eight years old.

The kid doesn't even know enough to take off his cap in the house.

Tufts of dark, unruly hair sprang from beneath the cap and over his ears.

Furthermore, he could use a haircut.

"I want you to meet my friend." The pastor put a hand on the boy's shoulder.

Becca could see the boy flinch.

By that time, she had reached the bottom of the stairs.

Is that all the stuff he's got? she thought, noticing the small sack of belongings at his feet.

Well, I guess he doesn't need much, seeing as he won't be staying long.

"How do you do?" she asked in her most cordial voice. Thirty verses were enough for one day.

The boy didn't respond, nor did he look at her. His chin touched his chest as he fixed his gaze on scuffed boots that looked to squeeze his feet.

"What's your name?" she asked.

Her question met with silence.

"Tell Becca your name, son," Pastor David urged.

The boy shook his head.

The pastor slid his arm around his shoulders. "This is Peter Chaloupek."

"Where does that name come from?" Becca asked, not unkindly.

"It's Czechoslovakian," the pastor said.

"Oh, I see. So he can't speak English."

Fierce, dark eyes met hers. "I—I c—c—can s—so."

He stutters. That's why he won't talk. Becca suppressed a twinge of sympathy.

"Peter was born in America. His parents both came from Czechoslovakia."

"We're so glad Peter will be visiting us, aren't we, Becca?" There was steel in her mother's tone as she moved to stand beside her husband.

Speak for yourself, Mama.

But it was a relief to hear her mother say "visit" instead of "reside." It sounded a lot less permanent.

Becca nodded.

"You're just in time for supper." Her mother's voice sounded gay, excessively so. "I've made a pot roast and mashed potatoes, along with some peas and corn that Becca and I canned, and an apple cobbler for dessert. How does that sound?"

The menu was obviously intended to entice the boy, but all her mother got was a sullen glance. She turned to the pastor. "Can you join us, David?"

Pastor David sniffed the wafting scent of the pot roast. "Wish I could, but old Steve Schultz is bad again. I promised to stop by." The pastor squatted down so he could look the boy in the face. "It's going to be all right, Peter. These are good folks."

Peter stood frozen. At least this time he didn't flinch when the pastor squeezed his shoulder.

"He'll be fine." Papa's voice was hardy with hope.

"Well, I'll be off then. I'll check back next week."

Next week?

Becca's heart sank. How long was he going to stay?

"Tell Sarah hello," her mother said as she and her husband walked Pastor David to the door and out onto the veranda—leaving Becca to entertain the boy.

She looked down at him and inwardly sighed. One of them had to say something, and it didn't look like there was much coming from him.

"Do you speak Czechoslovakian?"

He shook his head. "I o—only t—t—talk Am—Am. . ." He took a deep breath. "Americ—can."

Carrying on a conversation with this kid was not going to be easy. But at least he was trying. She had to give him that.

"My dad speaks German," Becca said. "His grandfather came over on a ship from Germany."

Over the boy's shoulder, she could see her parents through the window next to the front door. They were engaged in deep conversation with Pastor David. Her father frowned. Her mother pulled a handkerchief from her sleeve and dabbed her eyes. Becca would have liked to be a fly buzzing that exchange.

She looked back at the stutterer. Now what? She supposed school was a safe subject. "Daddy said you were my age. Ten."

He nodded.

"Then I guess you'll be in my grade at school. You'll like our teacher, Miss Jensen. She's nice."

At the mention of school, Becca saw the boy's face change from relative calm to anxious to downright stubborn.

Whoa, what have I said now?

"I—I don't g—g—go to school."

Becca crossed her arms. "You have to go to school. It's the law. Every kid has to go to school until the eighth grade."

"I—I d—d—don't." He stuck out his chin and glared up at her.

Becca tilted her naturally imperious nose. "We'll see."

"N—no! I w—won't. Nobody c—can make m—me." He was almost yelling now.

Well, at least it got the attention of those on the veranda. *Now maybe I'll get some help in here.*

Becca's father hurried down the steps with Pastor David. Her mother turned and bustled through the front door. She gave Becca a searching look—actually, a blaming look if one was to ask Becca.

Becca shrugged. "All I said was that we had to go to school."

"I a–ain't." Peter's voice was vehement.

"*I'm not*," Becca said, taking a perverse pleasure in correcting him.

"That's enough, Becca," her mother demanded. "Show Peter where to put his things. Dinner will be ready in half an hour."

The boy picked up his sack of belongings and followed Becca up the stairs and down the hall to the spare bedroom in the corner next to hers.

"This will be your room," she said, thrusting the door open, "while you're visiting."

She didn't want to give him any false expectations about how long he could expect to stay.

He stepped across the threshold but went no farther, as if he was almost afraid to enter. Slowly his eyes scanned the cheery room, studying each minute detail with infinite interest, as if he was consigning it to memory to pull out later and examine: the pale yellow walls, the bed with the patchwork quilt, the old pine dresser with the mirror above it, and the crocheted dresser scarf that matched the curtains at the window looking out to the orchard. He studied the bentwood rocker, Mama's sewing machine tucked into the corner, and her watercolors of flowers hanging on the walls—an art she had tried to pass on to Becca, without much success.

"It used to be the nursery," Becca said, "but now it's Mama's sewing room." *So don't get too comfortable,* she wanted to add, but she refrained. "We just use it as a bedroom when we have visitors."

For the longest time, he continued to stare, clutching his sorry sack of belongings and not saying a word. So absorbed was he that it was as if Becca weren't even there.

That he didn't speak was a relief and certainly no surprise.

What was a surprise was the expression of wonder in his large, dark eyes. As Becca watched him, it occurred to her that what she saw as her old nursery this orphan boy viewed as an oasis of peace in his troubled life.

She pointed to the dresser. "You can have the top drawers for your things. Mama uses the bottom two for her sewing. The outhouse is in the back behind the cottonwood tree, but you can wash up in the kitchen. My dad rigged up a pump inside."

She didn't want to feel sorry for him, but she couldn't help herself. He was so pinched and small, so obviously overwhelmed by all she took for granted.

That didn't mean she wanted him here, far from it. He and his stuttering were a nuisance. It just made it easier to make the best of things until Pastor David could find him a permanent home.

"I'm gonna help Mama in the kitchen. Come on down when you're ready."

The aroma of simmering pot roast and minted peas and the scent of cinnamon and apples wafted up the stairs as Becca descended, reminding her again of how seriously hungry she was. Worry and frustration had always fueled her appetite, and she could not remember a more worrisome or frustrating day than this.

She quickly set the table and lit the candles, while her mother brought the food from the stove, absently singing as she moved about. This time, " 'Come to the church in the wildwood. . .Ta-da-da-da-da. . .'" Down the middle of the table, she placed the platter of sliced roast surrounded by the onions softened in its juices, the boat of rich gravy made from the drippings. " '. . .in the vale. . .'" Then came the bowl of creamy white mashed potatoes with a dollop of butter dripping from the peak like a golden volcano, the minted peas, the corn, and a basket of flaky biscuits. " 'No spot is so dear to my childhood'—Call everybody to dinner," she ordered, removing her apron.

Which is exactly what Becca did, shouting loudly from the middle of the entry hall. "Dinner's served!"

Her mother poked her head out of the kitchen. "I didn't mean it literally, dear."

Becca grinned. "Too late."

Her father came out of the library and followed her down the hall to the kitchen where they settled into their usual places around the trestle table and waited for their guest— what else could he be called?—to join them.

"Well, wife, you've outdone yourself again." Her father smiled at Mama in that special way. "Indeed you've created a feast."

Becca's mother laughed and batted her lashes. "Pshaw, Jacob, you always say that."

"And I always mean it."

There was that moment between them that was just theirs, not even Becca was part of it. But rather than feeling left out, she found it comforting to be warmed in the glow of her parents' love for each other.

After a few minutes, her father said, "Do you think the boy heard you, Becca?"

"How could he not?" Her mother looked askance at her daughter. "I suspect they heard her in the next county. I'm sure he'll be down shortly."

But when several more minutes passed, it became obvious that he was not coming after all, and a disgruntled Becca was dispatched to fetch him.

He's only been here an hour, and already he's a pain, she thought as she clomped up the stairs.

The door to the sewing room was ajar. She peeked in. Through the rosy haze of twilight, she could see him curled up on the bed, his face toward the window. She crept over and tentatively touched his arm to see if he was awake.

He sprang to his feet so suddenly that he nearly knocked her down. "D–don't do tha–that," he snarled.

Becca jumped back, staring at him in disbelief, then turned

on her heel. "Dinner's on the table."

She stomped down the stairs, down the hall, into the kitchen, and plopped into her chair.

"Where's our guest?" her father asked.

"Hopefully, he's not coming down. And I say, good! No wonder he wasn't chosen. He's a vicious little animal."

Without a word, her father rose and disappeared into the hall. She could hear his footsteps on the stairs.

Ready to blame Becca, her mother frowned. "What happened?"

As Becca was explaining, her father reappeared, Peter in tow.

Becca glared as he slid into the empty chair across from her.

Peter glowered back.

He doesn't even take his cap off at the table. He'll get a tongue-lashing now, for sure.

She glanced at her mother. But her mother didn't seem to notice.

If it had been me, you would have noticed, all right. You would have cut off my head with the hat still on it.

The boy reached out and started to grab a biscuit from the basket in front of him.

At this, her mother did take note. She laid a gentle hand on his arm.

At least he didn't jerk away when she *touched him.*

"Here we say a blessing before we eat, Peter."

Becca bowed her head. She peeked beneath her lashes to see if he had gotten the message.

Apparently he had.

"Dear Lord, thank You for bringing Peter into our lives, for giving us this opportunity to make a new friend. . ."

Becca figured her mother's preamble was as much for her benefit as the kid's.

"And to share the blessings You have given us. . . ." Then, as the roast grew cold, she spent considerable time listing the blessings, the birds, the flowers. . . Finally, she concluded, "And thank You for this food, Lord. May it feed our bodies as

You feed our souls, giving us the strength to do the work You intend us to do. In Jesus' precious name. Amen."

At once the boy's hand shot out, and he grabbed the biscuit he'd dropped back into the basket. Without so much as a "Please pass me" or "Thank you," he began to load his plate with mashed potatoes, peas, and slices of meat. Like a person starved, he reached for more, even as he chewed.

"G–gravy." He pointed.

"*Please?*" Becca said.

Her mother shot her a threatening look.

Becca couldn't believe it.

If I behaved the way he's behaving, she'd have washed my mouth out with soap and cut off my hands. To say nothing of a lecture that would last from now 'til the flowers bloom in the spring.

But aside from the dirty looks she sent to Becca, her mother just went on eating as if the boy's behavior were absolutely normal.

"Is the room to your liking?" her father asked him.

The boy nodded, continuing to chew as gravy drooled down his chin.

It was disgusting.

When they had finished eating, Becca and her mother got up to clear the table. "Does apple cobbler sound good to you, Peter?" her mother asked.

Becca couldn't understand it. Her parents were being so blind to the kid's rude manners, his obnoxious behavior. So solicitous of his every wish, especially her mother, the tough, righteous disciplinarian.

As her mother dished up the cobbler and Becca served, her father attempted conversation—actually more of a soliloquy— with the boy.

Becca's own thoughts went back to her parents' conversation with Pastor David on the front veranda. At the time, she had wondered why her father was frowning and why her mother, who always managed to keep her emotions in check, pulled out her hankie and dabbed her eyes.

Becca sat down at the table. Absently she poured cream over her cobbler and picked up her spoon.

Clearly her mother and father had learned something about the boy that they had not shared with her.

three

In the middle of the night, Becca woke up. For some moments, she lay in her bed in that soft, slumbering state between wakefulness and sleep, and then she stirred and sat up.

The glow from a full moon poured through the window, painting her room and all its contents in burnished silver: the horses her daddy had whittled that sat on top of her bookcase, her canopied bed and rosebud coverlet, the dainty dresser that had once been her mother's, the intricately carved chest in which she kept her clothes, the cabbage roses on her papered walls. In this magic midnight light, her room looked like a fairyland. The same as it had for her mama. For with the exception of the horses and the wallpaper, it had been her mother's room as a girl, its contents shipped from Boston by her elegant grandmother Wilcox when Becca's mother had married Papa.

These were her mother's treasurers, and now they were hers. And Becca loved them, even though she might have chosen differently, given the choice.

But what had wakened her? She listened. Through the closed window, she heard the muffled clack of crickets. . .and something else. Sobbing, in the room next to hers.

And then the softly crooning voice of her mother.

Becca slipped from under the covers. As her bare feet touched the cold hardwood floor, she wrapped her arms around herself to hold in the warmth and tiptoed into the hall.

" 'What a friend we have in Jesus. . .' " Her mother's voice rang soft, sweet, and clear.

Becca peeked through the partially open door. Silhouetted against the window her mother rocked, Peter curled up in her arms.

Becca's heart twisted into a fist.

She belonged in her mother's arms, not this interloper, this puny, mean, obnoxious little kid who couldn't even get a word out edgewise.

Hot tears of jealousy and anguish sprang to her eyes.

There was something about the scene that looked much too permanent. The way her mother held him, brushed the hair from his brow like she always did with Becca, the way she bent and kissed his cheek and stroked his arm.

Her premonition had been right. What she was seeing confirmed her worst fears.

She would be stuck with him. Forever.

Sobbing, Becca ran back down the hall, dove into bed, and yanked the covers over her head.

It would serve them right if she ran away. Tomorrow she would run away. But they probably wouldn't even notice.

Angrily she swiped at her stupid tears and her running nose and sniffed.

And if they do notice, they won't care. They have him now. A son. A stupid son! They'll just change the sheets and move him into my room.

She couldn't stop the blubbering. It just welled up from deep inside, no matter how hard she tried to muffle it.

The mattress sank beside her. Her mother. She climbed under the covers next to Becca.

Mortified, Becca turned her back, swallowing the little hiccuping sobs that would not be suppressed, and lay rigid as her mother reached for her.

"Oh, Becca, I'm so sorry that you're sad," her mother whispered.

"You—you're going to keep him. I know you are."

"Oh, honey, my comforting Peter has nothing to do with that." Her mother laid her cheek against Becca's. "He's such a sad little fellow."

"Ten years old isn't little."

"It isn't for you. You have good food and strong bones and a loving family to take care of you. Peter isn't so lucky."

"Well, now he is."

"Only for the time being. Your daddy and I have always said you're enough for us."

Her mother released her and sat up. "Remember how Papa and I were talking to Pastor David on the veranda? I think you need to know what it was about."

Wiping away the wetness, Becca rolled over on her back so she could look up at her mother.

She smoothed Becca's hair as she spoke. "You've never been to a city—"

"I've been to Whispering Bluff."

"Whispering Bluff is a town—and a very small one. I'm talking about a very big city. New York. Peter's mama and papa came to New York from far away—"

"Czechoslovakia."

"That's right, Czechoslovakia. When they got here, they didn't speak any English, which made it hard for them to get work, and even when they did, they didn't make much money. Barely enough for food. And then Peter was born, and then came his little sister."

"Peter has a sister?"

Her mother shook her head sadly. "Not anymore."

"What happened?"

"Shh." Her mother laid a finger on Becca's lips. "I'm getting to that. New York is a very big, very dirty, very crowded city. Even dirtier and more crowded in the slums where the poorest people live. And Peter's family was very, very poor. They lived in a tenement. All four of them in one room, with another family."

"What's a tenement?"

"It's a tall wooden building with many floors where lots of families live, and so crowded that. . . Well, you know how tight we pack the cucumbers when we're making pickles?"

"That squished in?" It was hard to believe. "A tenement is *that* crowded?"

"Almost. And with that many people squeezed together, there are bound to be lots of accidents and fires. And if there's a fire in a tenement, it goes up fast, like the kindling in our fireplace, too fast for people to escape. Many die."

Becca sat up. "Is that what happened to Peter's family?"

"Yes," her mother said softly, putting her arm around Becca's shoulder and pulling her close. "On that terrible day, Peter had gone out selling matches, shining shoes, anything to get a little extra money to help. When he came home, all that was left was the charred skeleton of the building. The rest was a pile of smoldering rubble. His whole family, his mama and daddy, his little sister, all were lost."

"They all died?" Becca could feel the sting of tears again. "Oh, Mama, how sad. Peter was alone. So that's how he ended up on the orphan train."

"No, not yet. He was so sad and so afraid he didn't know what to do. He didn't want to go to an orphanage. He'd heard bad things about the orphanages. So at first he hid, sleeping in alleys and abandoned buildings. He just roamed the streets, doing odd jobs like peddling newspapers or picking coal, running errands. But he made only a few pennies a day. If he was lucky."

"Was that enough to buy food?"

"No. He searched through garbage cans for food."

"That's how he ate? No wonder his table manners are so bad. I'll bet our dinner was the best he's ever had."

"I wouldn't be surprised. When he thought he was safe, he went back to the shell of that burned-out tenement. In the summer, it was hot and sticky, and in the winter, he nearly froze."

"You still haven't told me how he got on the orphan train."

"It was last winter that he found a place to stay called Children's Aid Society where the homeless children in New York can live. They get medical care there, and warm food and clothing. A minister named Charles Loring Brace started it, and he doesn't believe in orphanages, either. He thinks children should be in families. Peter is one of the children he sent west to find a family."

Becca and her mother were silent for some time, each thinking her own thoughts.

Finally, Becca murmured, "I think I still want to be your only kid, Mama. Is that selfish?"

"You are our only 'kid' and always will be." Her mother planted a kiss on her forehead. "If someone else were to enter our lives, it would be a decision you and Papa and I would make together."

A great sense of relief rolled over Becca. She trusted her mother. She knew Mama would always tell her the truth, even when it wasn't something Becca wanted to hear.

Becca cuddled closer and looked up at her. "I'm glad you told me about Peter. Now that I understand, I think I can be nicer to him."

"You're such a compassionate, kind person, I have no doubt." Her mother gave her a hug. "I don't think we need to discuss any of this with him, however, or anybody else. Do you? He might be embarrassed."

"It'll just be our secret. I won't even tell Jane." Jane was Becca's best friends. "But I know she'll be kind, too."

"I'm sure of it. That's the sort of youngster she is."

※

It happened that all the orphan train children taken into the Whispering Bluff-area families were either babies or toddlers. Older children had gone into farm families in outlying districts with the intention they be included in family activities, help with the daily chores, and learn skills they could use later.

At church that Sunday, Peter stood out not only because of his age or his ill-fitting clothes but for his sullen reticence, as well. Even when Pastor David greeted him, his gaze skirted from the pastor's kind eyes as he mumbled a response. In church he sat between Becca and her mother, and when Becca tried to share the hymnal, he turned his face away.

He sure makes it hard to feel sorry for him, Becca thought.

Following the service, the ladies had prepared a potluck lunch in the church basement. Planks were set on sawhorses and covered with yards of red-and-white gingham; the makeshift tables' centerpieces were baskets of apples. There were plain wood benches on either side for folks to sit.

A long table near the entrance was laden with baskets of homemade bread, platters of sliced cheese and ham, fried chicken, casseroles of rabbit stew, deviled eggs, bowls of potato salad, beans and corn, preserved tomatoes, cucumbers, pies of all kinds, and bread pudding with molasses sauce. Becca's favorite.

Pastor David blessed the orphan train children and the families that had welcomed them, adding thanks for the food and the loving hands that had prepared it. Then, much to Becca's relief, the ladies stood behind the table and served each person in line. Peter's unschooled manners would have brought disconcerting attention if he had been allowed to grab his choices.

"Love your new dress, Becca." Balancing a full plate, Jane McKee, Becca's best friend, paused on her way from the buffet table.

Jane was the genteel girl Becca's mother should have had, all blond curls and dimples, ruffles and lace. Jane's mother had died in childbirth, leaving her father, the sheriff of Whispering Bluff, to raise her.

When Becca's mother was able, she acted as Jane's substitute mother. The relationship was rewarding to them both, since Jane was more amenable to learning the womanly arts than Becca and loved wearing the pretty outfits Becca's mother took such joy in creating for her.

Becca set her plate down on the table and slid into the seat Jane had saved for her.

"You didn't tell me your family was going to take in an orphan," Jane said.

"Only temporarily," Becca said with guilty relief.

Her mother and father arrived and sat down on the bench beside her, crowding Peter in next to Becca, who introduced him to Jane.

Jane leaned forward, smiling. "Hi, Peter. Welcome."

Peter didn't acknowledge her greeting. The instant his bottom had hit the bench, he'd dug into his plate of food with the same embarrassing vigor demonstrated the night before. It was almost as if he inhaled it.

Jane's eyes met Becca's.

Becca shrugged.

Peter had cleaned his plate and polished off two pieces of pie while Becca's parents were still on their salads. He sat at the table, his hands clutched in his lap, staring at his empty plate.

Jane tried again. "I've never ridden on a train, Peter. Was it fun?"

Peter shrugged.

"Where did you come from?"

"N–N–New York," he mumbled.

"That's a long way away. How many days did it take to get here?"

"A–a–about e–eight d–d–days."

The twelve-year-old Singleton twins who had been listening to the conversation began to giggle.

"You talk funny," Lucy Singleton said.

Bitsy Singleton laughed. "Maybe that's the way they all talk in New York."

Becca could feel Peter's body tense beside her. A blush traveled up his face. His dark eyes took on the fierce glint she'd seen the night before.

"Don't pay any attention to them, Peter. They're stupid," she said in a tone that carried across the table.

"We are not stupid," Bitsy said, her voice rising.

"Not only are they stupid, but they're mean," Becca said.

Jane chimed in. "You can say that again."

"Mrs. Hostettler, Becca called Bitsy and me stupid," Lucy tattled.

Before her mother could respond, Becca and Jane had jumped up from the table and picked up their plates. "Come along, Peter." Casting a withering glance in the twins' direction, Becca gathered up his plate, as well. "We need some fresh air."

With her two companions in tow, Becca, nose in the air, strode away.

Later, though, when the family was climbing into the buggy to go home, her mother turned to Becca with a stern expression. "Becca, you know very well we do not call people stupid. . .even when they are."

❧

The next morning, Becca's mother burst into Becca's bedroom just as she was finishing lacing up her shoes.

"I can't find him anywhere. Peter's gone. Oh dear." She wrung her hands. "I'm sure it's because I said he had to go to school."

"I can't imagine that would be the reason, Mama." Becca jumped up from the chair in front of her vanity. "I told him that myself."

"Oh, Becca, last night, he confessed that he can't read. He was afraid that everyone would make fun of him. I assured him it wasn't so, but I guess he didn't believe me." She turned, distraught. "Run and tell your father he's run away. We've got to find him."

At that moment, they heard the kitchen door slam. They looked at each other and made a beeline for the stairs.

"Where's our breakfast?" her father called. "You've got two hungry farmers down here!"

Becca and her mother burst into the kitchen to find Peter and her father side by side at the pump, washing their hands.

"Look who I found raking the empty stalls when I went out to do my chores at five o'clock." Her father smiled down at the boy. "I think I've found myself a real farmhand here."

"I–I'm a g–g–good w–worker even i–if I c–can't r–r–read. A–ain't I, Unc–uncle J–Jacob?"

"You are, indeed, Peter." Her father patted his shoulder.

The boy gazed at him with a face so filled with hope and

longing that even Becca's heart was touched.

Wait a minute!

Uncle Jacob?

Suddenly, she didn't know whether to be relieved that he hadn't run away or even more concerned at the ever increasing possibility that he would become a permanent fixture.

After breakfast, instead of riding her horse to school, Becca's father drove her in the buggy. He arranged with the teacher, Miss Jensen, that Peter could be homeschooled until he had the rudiments of reading. That afternoon, she sent Becca home with copies of *McGuffey's Eclectic Reader*, a *Youth's Companion* magazine, and a spelling book.

Peter's appetite for learning turned out to be as voracious as his appetite for food. He was insatiable. With the family's help, in no time he was almost up to grade in *McGuffey's Eclectic Reader*, and in addition, he'd mastered simple stories in Becca's book of Bible stories for children.

As he learned to read, a whole world opened up for him. He poured over Papa's almanacs and sounded out words in the dictionary. And he remembered everything, down to the minutest detail.

Becca listened and learned, too, as her father, with infinite patience, sat beside him in the evening after dinner, explaining the meaning of the words Peter didn't understand.

Each day, when Becca came home from school, Mama insisted they do their studies side by side at the kitchen table. To her surprise, a bond began to form between them.

It was no more than two months until Peter scrambled up behind Becca on her horse, Pegasus, for his first day of school.

The white frame, one-room schoolhouse served grades one through eight. The double desks circled a potbellied stove in the middle of the room. The children faced the front where Miss Jensen sat on a small platform, a large blackboard behind her. Since there were only fourteen students, each worked independently and received individual attention from the teacher.

"Children, please welcome your new classmate, Peter Chaloupek," Miss Jensen said.

A loud guffaw came from the back of the room. "It quacks, it snaps, it must be a Chaloupek." This from the class bully, Buddy Singleton, who was taking sixth grade for the second time and was large for his age anyway. He had everyone in the school intimidated, even Miss Jensen, although she obviously tried to put up a brave front.

"That will be enough, Buddy," she said in a stern but slightly wavering voice.

That first recess, the line was drawn—but not in the direction anyone expected.

It was as if the Singletons had been lying in wait.

"Th–th–there's the b–boy that t–talks funny," Lucy Singleton snorted.

"W–w–with th–the f–f–funny n–name," Bitsy sneered.

Peter shouted, "Y–you t–take that b–back!" his twiggy legs apart, his fists clenched.

Buddy Singleton trotted over and gave him a shove. "You don't talk to my sister that way, you little twit."

Fury fueled Becca's courage. "Don't you touch him."

"Well, look who's talking." Buddy Singleton pranced around her, slapping the air with a limp wrist.

Jane ran up and locked her arms with Becca's. "Mind your own business, Buddy."

"Oh, so now the baby needs two nursemaids." Buddy gave Peter another shove just for good measure.

The angry girls moved toward him. But to their surprise, Peter jumped in front of them.

His large, dark eyes glittered like pieces of smoldering coal. His face, fiery red. "I—I c–c–can t–take care of m–myself," he spat at them.

Buddy Singleton, half a head taller and twice as heavy, began to laugh. He grabbed the collar of Peter's shirt, lifting him off the ground.

For an instant, Peter dangled; then, with a mighty twist, he yanked away, leaving a handful of his torn collar in the bully's hand.

"Why, you little..." Buddy lunged for him.

But Peter was wily and quick. Obviously lessons learned on the streets of New York had not been lost on him. He dodged back, sprinted forward, then to the side. Darting and dipping like a dervish, he whirled around the brute, feinting to the left, feinting to the right. Suddenly, with a move too quick to catch, his fist sprang out, finding its mark on Buddy Singleton's chin. Buddy staggered back. The second blow sent him sprawling.

In an instant, Peter was on top of him, battering the bully's arms, pummeling his chest. "D—do you g—g—give? Do y—you g—give?"

Blood dripped from Buddy Singleton's nose. Tears made rivulets down his dirt-encrusted cheeks. "I give," he cried weakly, covering his head with his arms.

It was at that moment Miss Jensen scurried down the steps. "Boys, boys, stop this fighting at once."

Minutes before, Becca was almost sure she had seen Miss Jensen's shadow at the classroom window. Had their teacher waited just long enough to see the outcome of the altercation before she interfered?

From that day until the last first grader in that school year had graduated, until Miss Jensen married and was no longer their teacher, Peter Chaloupek would be enshrined in the hearts of them all as the boy who brought Buddy, the bully, down.

Except, of course, for the Singletons.

four

May 1898

A twilight sun slanted through the kitchen windows, painting rectangles on the oak floor and the trestle table holding the last remnants of supper.

Jacob leaned back in his chair. "How many springs since you joined this family, Peter? Six?"

"Seven. Seven years of paradise, Uncle Jacob." Peter smiled at the man who had been like a father to him. More than that, he had been a mentor and friend. Compared to Peter's prior life—the teeming streets of New York when he was "little Petrov"—this farm outside Whispering Bluff, Colorado, was indeed paradise.

In fact, the past had dimmed to a dream so remote it could have happened to someone else. But then, at odd moments, when he was watching a sunset over the gently rolling sea of prairie grass or in the silver stillness of dawn just as he started his morning chores, a scene would flash before his eyes, so vivid it sparked a visceral response: a stomach cramped with hunger, the blister of hot pavements in summer, the bluster of winter with rags for a blanket; the squalor, the stink, the noise. His family. . .lost. The fear.

"It's hard to remember when you weren't with us," Jacob said.

"Not for me." Across the table Becca made a face at him. "Puny, pathetic little Peter got all the attention. Still does, for that matter."

Faith gave her daughter a sideways glance as she lifted her cup of tea. "I'd hardly call him puny or pathetic now."

"Or little," Jacob added. "He's taller than you, Becca."

"By an eyebrow," Becca retorted.

"And growing." Peter reached over and spooned another helping of cobbler—his third.

"Your table manners could still use some work." Becca licked the back of her spoon.

"As could yours," he observed before her mother could correct her. He helped himself to the cream.

Jacob laughed. "And now you are both about to graduate from high school."

"First and second in our class," Peter reminded him with a grin.

Becca gave him a narrowed look. "Okay, Mr. Pretending-to-be-Modest, we all know you're number one. But who was it who taught you everything you know?"

"Your father."

"That's not fair. Every night at this very table, I—"

"Don't get all riled up, dulcet girl—"

"I hate it when you call me that. Sweet's the last thing I am."

"You know I give credit where it's due." His face turned serious. "You were always my advocate and champion."

"Even when you didn't want me to be."

He looked at her fondly. "Most of the time I did. . .do."

Becca captured the last bit of peach syrup in the bottom of her bowl. "You forgot to mention it is I who was chosen class valedictorian."

"Only because you don't stutter when you get nervous."

"You don't stutter anymore, Peter," Faith said. "At least not enough to notice."

"And," Becca continued, "because I'm prettier than you."

"I have my following."

"If you call the Singleton twins a following."

Faith feigned disgust and poured herself another cup of tea. "You children."

Becca glanced over at her father. "Obviously, Papa, you haven't told Mama yet."

Faith looked from one to the other. "Secrets, you two?"

"You're a big girl, Becca. It's up to you to tell her," her father said.

"Tell me what?"

Peter braced for what was coming.

Becca straightened in her chair and locked her hands in her lap. "I applied to the university—"

"You *what?*"

"I've always said I wanted to go. You know that, Mama."

"That was a little girl's dream, not a woman's."

"It's not a dream."

Faith frowned at Jacob. "Surely you didn't encourage her in this."

"Papa didn't know. I sent the application on my own."

"Without discussing it with your parents? You know very well I've—we've—been looking into that fine Christian finishing school in Denver."

"Like the one you went to in Boston." Becca rolled her eyes.

"Becca...," her father warned.

"I'm sorry, Papa, but I just can't see myself at some hoity-toity finishing school where I learn to lift my pinky when I sip a cup of tea."

"You know very well that's not at all what it's like," Faith fumed. "We learned Christian values and standards based on the Bible. The foundation for our future lives and those of our children."

Peter could sense a speech coming.

"In addition, we studied the womanly arts of homemaking, decorating, fashion, manners, gracious entertaining—"

"All of which you've certainly been able to put to good use as a farmer's wife," Becca muttered.

"I'm warning you," her father said.

"It wasn't just the womanly arts—although *you* could certainly use a dose of them. Every morning, we went to chapel—twice on Sundays—and had daily Bible study. We developed standards of behavior and intelligent conversation. We studied

literature and music and art. That's where I learned to paint."
Her mother glowered at her. "Don't give me that look, my girl.
You'd do well with some polish. A fine Christian finishing
school is not fluff; it prepares a young lady for a productive
Christian life."

"I've been living in a Christian finishing school for seventeen years, Mama, with you." Becca crossed her arms and
looked belligerently at her mother. "It's about time I branched
out into the real world. I want to do something important
with my life."

"Being a good wife and mother isn't important?"

"That's not what I said. We just want different things in
life, that's all."

Peter could see Faith's mind working behind her steely
expression and glittering eyes. A new approach was forming.
Her face softened. More conciliatory. She reached out her
hand.

"Part of it is, I don't want to see you disappointed, Becca.
You know how difficult it is for a woman to get into the
university."

"Does that mean I shouldn't try? Or maybe you don't think
I'm smart enough."

"Of course you're smart enough. But you're refusing to
face the obvious. You're a woman, a beautiful young woman
with more beaux than you can count. Before long you'll be
married. You'll be responsible for being a helpmate to your
husband and raising children in the ways of the Lord. The
Bible says—"

"I know what the Bible says. You've been quoting it to me
all my life."

"Don't speak to your mother in that tone." Jacob started to
rise, but Faith gestured him back.

"The Bible says," she continued, " 'She looketh well to the
ways of her household, and eateth not the bread of idleness.
Her children arise up, and call her blessed; her husband also,
and he praiseth her.'"

No one spoke.

It was hard to argue with the Bible.

They all looked at Becca, and Becca, unmoved, stared at her empty plate.

Faith shook her head and sighed. "You don't think I understand, Becca, but I do, more than you know. Believe it or not, when I was young I had my dreams, too. In those days it was even harder for a woman to get an education than it is now. But like you, I was determined. It was my father who convinced me otherwise." She looked pointedly at Jacob.

He quirked a brow. "And all this time I thought it was because a tall, handsome, debonair young man swept you off your feet."

"Don't make light of this, Jacob," Faith said severely.

Becca sat in belligerent silence.

"I'd like to hear from you, Miss Becca." Faith waited.

"If you're so doubtful I'll be accepted to the university, I don't know why we're having this conversation."

Jacob shook his head.

He was deeply fond of his daughter, but he recognized her willful ways. In fact, he had even confessed to Peter that he felt Faith and he had given in to Becca much too often. He was afraid, he said, that someday they would have to pay for it. Looking from Uncle Jacob to the determined Aunt Faith to the resolute Becca, it appeared that day had arrived.

"You're right. This conversation is over." Faith pushed her chair back from the table. But she couldn't let it drop. "If you're so against a genteel education, you could go to normal school, become a teacher in two years. At least that would be practical."

"They don't teach veterinary medicine at normal school."

"*Veterinary medicine?* That's what you want to study? How to drench sheep and deliver calves? Well, that's certainly an appropriate career for a woman." Faith had given it her all, and it hadn't done a lick of good. An angry red stained her cheeks; her slender hands trembled. "And if, per chance, you *are* accepted to the university, who, pray tell, is going to finance this extravagance?"

"It wouldn't be an extravagance if Peter chose to go to college," Becca declared angrily.

"You know money isn't an issue, Faith," Jacob's voice was calm.

"Whose side are you on?" Faith spat.

Peter was surprised that Jacob's response had not been more forceful. Was it possible that he did not wholly share his wife's resolve? Could he secretly favor Becca's attending the university? He had always treated Peter and Becca equally, never making special compensation for her because she was a girl—often to the consternation of his wife.

"I'll use my inheritance from Grandma Wilcox," Becca interjected.

Faith's voice shook. "My mother would turn over in her grave. She left that money for your trousseau." She shot her husband a betrayed glare. "How can you let this happen?" Pursing her lips, she turned suddenly to Peter. "Were you in on this?"

Peter swallowed. Aunt Faith might be frail in body but certainly not in spirit. He had not forgotten those rare occasions when he had suffered her wrath.

"Don't bother to answer. Your face says it all."

Becca pushed her chair away from the table and stood up. "I knew it would be like this, Mother. That's why I didn't want to tell you." She threw her napkin on the table.

"Sit down!" Faith gave her daughter a look Becca dared not disobey.

She dropped back into her chair, her jaw clenched, her slate eyes focused on the plate in front of her. White-knuckled fingers clutched the chair's arms.

She might look like her father, but she had her mother's volatile temperament.

"You are an obstinate, disobedient girl," Faith exclaimed, "and I pity the man who marries you!"

A heavy silence fell over the table, broken only by the slam of the screen door caught in a sudden breeze.

Faith finally spoke. "I'm sorry I said that." She looked over at her daughter, but there was little contrition in her face. "The part about pitying the man you marry—not the part about your being obstinate and disobedient."

Becca bolted to her feet, as did her father. But she would not be stilled. "Just so you know, finishing school would be wasted on me since I don't intend *ever* to get married." She turned—with a dramatic flourish, Peter observed—and ran from the room, tears coursing down her cheeks.

Faith looked first at Jacob and then at Peter. "Am I all alone here?"

Neither met her eyes.

five

In the waning light of evening, Becca lay on the crumpled coverlet, her skirt askew, her curls spread over the pillow in a tangled mass. Bitter tears burned her eyes, ran down her cheeks, dampening the down pillow beneath her head.

How could they? They, who had always encouraged her to take chances, grasp opportunities. "*Carpe diem*—seize the day," Papa always said. Now, when she'd done that, demonstrated the very attributes they applauded—initiative, tenacity, ambition—they had denied her.

Becca couldn't believe it.

And all because Mama was convinced that Becca needed training in the "womanly arts."

Womanly arts. The expression made her gag!

It wasn't that she didn't enjoy being a girl. She did. She loved having lots of beaux. Preened in their compliments. Even when she knew they were exaggerating.

"You have more valuable assets than beauty," Mama always said, not wanting to encourage Becca's vanity. "You have intelligence and taste. A way with words."

"A compassionate soul," her father would add.

As a result, Becca had confidence, supreme and utter confidence instilled by her parents' belief and trust.

And now they were snatching it all away.

It was as if they had suddenly bound her feet, her hands. . . her heart.

She flung an arm over her eyes, about to go into another torrent of tears, when a knock sounded at the bedroom door.

"Becca, it's me, Peter. May I come in?" His voice was deep and confident, not like a boy's anymore.

She hesitated, wondering if even he could comfort her at a

time like this, when her whole world was collapsing around her. "If you must," she mumbled.

"I must."

The door opened, and he stood silhouetted in the dusk, tall—well, almost tall—tousled hair, broad shoulders, substantial, and safe. Probably the only person who really could understand how she was suffering.

He strode across the room with lanky grace, cowboy boots clacking on the hardwood floor, and dropped down on the edge of the bed, his weight bouncing the mattress.

"How could they do this to me? Papa especially. I expected him to be on my side." Becca sniffed, wiping her nose with the back of her hand. "At least Mama's consistent, still trying to make a lady of me. She probably thinks it's her last chance. Oh, Peter," she wailed. "What am I going to do?"

He gazed down at her, his square-jawed, even-featured face radiating the comfort that she needed. "All is not lost."

"What do you mean?" She swung her legs to the floor and sat up beside him.

"As we speak, I suspect your father is trying to convince your mama to let things take their course."

"Do you think so?" She grabbed his arm.

"I know so. They went into the library—"

"You listened."

"I wouldn't do such a thing. I just happened to be walking past. . .slowly. . .several times."

"So, what did he say?"

"That they'd brought you up to follow your heart and ought to give you the chance to do it."

"What did Mama say?"

"I couldn't hear. She was talking kinda quiet." His straight, white teeth gleamed in a teasing smile. "But I'd say it sounded hopeful."

Becca slumped. "I don't trust Mama; the more determined she is, the quieter she gets."

Peter dropped an arm around her shoulders and gave her

a consoling squeeze. "Don't be too hard on her, Becca; she'd do anything for you. Even if she is misguided, she loves you a lot."

"Misguided to love me a lot, or misguided in what she does?"

"You know what I mean."

"Sometimes I think she loves me *too* much. She wants me to be perfect." Becca screwed up her face. "As she perceives perfection."

Peter had no comeback this time. He just sat there.

He knows I'm right!

She plopped back onto the bed and looked up in silence at the ceiling. Finally she said, "You could go to college, Peter. Mama and Papa would pay for it in a minute."

"I wouldn't feel right. They've done so much for me already."

"You know they think of you as a son." She gave his arm an encouraging squeeze. "I think of you as a brother."

Peter shifted his gaze to hers, his dark, gentle eyes suddenly inscrutable. Then he leaned forward, balancing his elbows on his knees, his strong, calloused hands locked together in front of him. "The truth is, I'm happy where I am," he said quietly. "Uncle Jacob needs me. It's a good feeling to be needed. . .to be wanted." He paused. "As for college, my college is right here, in your father's library. If I read every book on those shelves, I'd be the best-educated man in the county."

"You really feel that way, don't you?"

He nodded. "I do."

"You're lucky. My heart is so restless. Sometimes I feel almost desperate, as if there's not enough time to see all the things I want to see, do all the things I want to do. For you it's so simple. It's all here."

He looked down at her and smiled. "Yes. I've seen all I ever want to see out there."

"If it weren't for you, Peter, I don't know how I could stand it."

❧

So, for the better part of that week and the next, a tenuous truce existed between parent and child. Becca understood her mother's quiet determination. Mama was not one to give in easily when she thought she was right. Nor was Becca.

Finally, after many heated discussions and much prayerful consideration, her mother released the matter to God, concluding that the outcome of Becca's application to the university was part of His plan for her daughter's life.

If Becca were accepted, her mother would rejoice.

"If not, however," her mother said, "it will be God's way of telling you that you should go to finishing school in Denver."

Vacillating between angst and optimism, Becca agreed to the terms. What other choice did she have?

Now it was a matter of patience. An attribute of which she held in short supply. And prayer, much prayer, that God would see she was right. Be on her side.

&

It was a crisp Saturday morning several weeks later. The chores were finished. In the kitchen, Mama and Helga Springer were canning the first pickling crop of green beans. Helga, a sturdy, middle-aged widow with five youngsters to support, had worked off and on for the Hostettlers since Peter joined the family.

Becca and Peter were in the barn nursing a sick calf while Papa sat on a bench outside repairing Pegasus's broken halter.

Peter stood and brushed the straw off his jeans. "I reckon you should be getting your acceptance from the university soon."

"I wish I had your confidence." Becca extended a hand to have him help her up, when a cry came from across the yard.

"Mr. Jacob! Mr. Jacob!"

Becca and Peter ran to the barn door. Helga was running toward them, her arms flailing, her flapping white apron splattered with red.

"The missus fell. She's hurt bad."

Across the yard Becca spotted her mother sprawled on the ground at the foot of the kitchen steps, her right leg twisted beneath her.

By the time Becca and Peter reached her, her father was already kneeling at his wife's side. Blood was everywhere, soaking her mother's apron, splashed on the wooden stairs, oozing into a crimson pool on the earth beside her.

A fist of dread clutched Becca's heart.

By now Helga had ripped off her apron and was struggling to stem the flow surging from a long angry gash on her mother's calf.

"I. . .I think my leg's broken," her mother gasped, clutching her husband's hand.

Becca could see that the wound was far worse than just a broken leg.

"You'll be all right, Faith. Don't worry." Her father reached down to lift her but was stopped by Helga's command.

"Don't touch her until we stabilize the leg." Instinctively the housekeeper seemed to understand what was needed.

The mother of five had seen it all, but had she seen anything as bad as this?

Becca paced, frightened and helpless. "Tell me what to do."

"We'll get her in the house first. Then there'll be plenty to do." Helga turned to her father. "Mr. Jacob, you support the missus' leg while Peter carries her. Careful there," she said, continuing to hold her blood-soaked apron against the wound while Peter and her father struggled to coordinate their efforts.

Becca held open the back door as they made their way up the steps, through the kitchen, and into the adjacent bedroom.

"Now, Becca, get me all the towels you can find. Mr. Jacob, we need hot water. Peter, you phone Doc Warner. We need him out here *now!*"

Helga tended the wound, while Becca ran back and forth, carrying fresh towels, filling tubs with hot water, rinsing linens. Her father added his strength to the tasks when he could, but most of the time he hovered over his beloved wife, wiping her brow, grasping her hand, murmuring words of encouragement.

Peter stuck his head through the bedroom door. "Doc Warner's in north county. Jake Spooner's little girl's taken sick again, and there's no telephone out there. It's at least three hours away." His cowboy hat was already clamped on his head. "I'll saddle up."

Before Becca could turn around, she heard the back door slam.

"I'm sorry. . .I'm so sorry. . .so sorry," her mother intoned, her voice hardly above a breath.

"Oh, my dear, don't say that." Distraught, her father leaned close, brushing back a strand of damp hair clinging to her brow.

Her mother moaned.

"We need an antiseptic," Helga said in a hushed tone. "Mr. Jacob, fetch some turpentine."

"It'll burn like crazy!" Becca hissed.

"It's the best we got." Helga's expression was grim.

"When I sprained my ankle, Doc Warner gave me laudanum. It helped with the pain," Becca said.

"Good thinking, girl."

"I'll see if we have some left." Becca was already hurrying from the room.

Despite all their efforts, the flow of blood could not be controlled.

"What are we going to do?" Becca whispered, wringing her hands.

"We'll try packing it with ashes. Maybe that'll stop it."

If only the doctor were here, there wouldn't be a *maybe*. He would know exactly what to do to help Mama. He would have the instruments they needed. The medicine they needed.

Where was he?

As the hours passed, Becca watched her mother's condition worsen. Her face grew paler, and yet she burned with fever. Helga had Becca brew sassafras tea, and she and her father wrapped Mama in damp sheets to try to bring the fever down.

Would they never get here? Peter had left at ten in the

morning. It was almost six and almost dark.

Then seven. . .nine. . .

Hour after hour, she, her father, and Helga repeated their endless ministrations.

And still no Peter. No doctor.

It seemed all they could do now was keep Mama comfortable.

Becca supported her mother's head, patiently spooning sassafras tea between her parched lips as Helga continued to tend the wound. Her father knelt beside the bed, grasping his wife's limp hand, praying and murmuring words of encouragement that Becca feared her mother could not hear.

Was it possible, she thought, that just hours ago the sun had risen as usual, that the family had joined together for morning prayers and breakfast, that her mother's absent hymn-humming had filled the kitchen as she went about her morning tasks?

And now she was struggling for her life.

Struggling for her life!

The impact of those words suddenly hit her full force.

She had been so engrossed in what needed to be done to keep her alive that it had never occurred to her that they would not succeed. That her mother might die.

Suddenly she found herself angry with Peter for not being there. She knew it made no sense, but she couldn't help it. This was where he belonged, to help them as he always did, and comfort them as he always had. Her mother was the spine of the family; her father, the gentle mediator; Peter, the rock on which they all leaned.

Where was he? Where was the doctor?

"I think I see them." Her father turned from the window.

Sassafras tea sloshed into the saucer as Becca set the cup on the bedside table and ran to see for herself.

Yes. Up the road. A light. The carriage light on Doc Warner's buggy. It had to be.

Within minutes, she heard the clatter of buggy wheels by the back door. A horse's neigh. Footsteps on the stairs.

Peter burst into the room, the bewhiskered doctor close behind him.

At last!

Peter was here.

Becca's pent-up emotions flooded through her. Now she could let go. She sagged against the bedpost.

Everything would be all right.

six

Peter sat across from Becca at the kitchen table, as he had that morning. But then the room had been saturated with sunshine and the smells of frying bacon and baking biscuits, the air filled with birdsong coming from the branches of the early blooming peach tree outside the kitchen window. Now the room was dim and still, save for the spit of cinders and the light from a waning fire on the grate.

Helga moved to the fireplace to stir the coals and add another log.

As Peter gazed on Becca's bowed head, his heart was filled with the anguish of despair and helplessness. He covered her hand. She turned it, grasping his. The gaze she lifted held little hope.

Beside him at the table, Jacob's head rested on his folded arms.

This family, now Peter's own, had done so much for him. Yet in their greatest need, he could do nothing for them but wait.

It wasn't long before the door to the bedroom opened and Doc Warner emerged, his shoulders sagging with weariness.

Becca leaped to her feet.

The doctor took her hand. "Such a nasty wound, Becca. You and Helga did an amazing job of taking care of her. There's little more I could have done."

Becca's face lit with hope. "Then Mama'll be all right?"

Peter sensed Doc Warner's hesitation, a mustering of his courage as he laid his hand on her shoulder. "Those faint red strands traveling up her leg are the sign of blood poisoning, Becca."

Jacob moaned, collapsing back into his chair. Becca grabbed the doctor's hands. "Surely there's something you can do?"

50

The old doctor's face reflected his compassion. "Under other circumstances I might be able to amputate. But she's lost so much blood, and with her frail heart, her body couldn't stand the shock."

Becca stared at the doctor, her head to the side, as if she couldn't quite understand. Then with a choking cry, she swayed toward her father.

Peter caught her as she collapsed.

He held her against him, held her tight, absorbing her shuddering sobs into himself. His own grief lost in hers.

Helga dropped into the chair Becca had vacated, crying into the corner of her apron.

Fighting his own tears, Peter bit into his lower lip, flinching as his teeth broke the flesh, tasting the salt of blood. How could he help Becca if he couldn't control his own emotions?

He felt the wetness of Becca's tears on his cheek, her damp, tangled curls against his hand. He wanted to comfort her, but try as he might, the words would not come. He could only remain mute in his own distress and grief.

Doc Warner sat down beside Jacob, his presence scant comfort in this kitchen filled with the quiet sobs of the distraught family.

Jacob lifted his head. He wiped his eyes with his damp handkerchief and blew his nose. "Is she awake? Can we speak to her?"

"Yes," the doctor said.

"How much time does she have?"

"Not much, I'm afraid."

"Does she know?"

He nodded. "When you're ready, she wants to see you."

Jacob stared down at his own trembling hands, his strong, vital body now slumped like an ancient in the chair. He struggled to his feet.

Becca's sobs had eased, although the tears continued to flow as she leaned into Peter, supported by his strength.

Jacob took her arm, and they moved to the bedroom door,

their steps slow with a hesitation born of apprehension and despair.

Peter stood in the doorway as Becca and her father approached the bed.

A kerosene lamp on the dresser bathed the bed in a muted glow, casting the rest of the room's contents in shadow. In the dim light, it was difficult to make out the mound of Faith's frail body beneath the patchwork quilt. Her golden hair, grown silver in the passing years, spread across the pillow—*like a halo*, Peter thought.

As Becca and Jacob drew close, her eyes lifted. She raised a frail hand. "Becca, Jacob. . . Where is Peter? I want you all with me." Her voice was soft but amazingly clear.

Even on her deathbed, she includes me.

Becca reached back for his hand and drew him into the sad circle.

Faith spoke to each of them in turn, her whispered words barely audible at times but filled with the passion of her heart. To Peter, she told of her love, her pride in his accomplishments, her confidence that the Lord would fulfill all his needs.

He shuddered with unspent tears until he felt Jacob's comforting arm and Becca's head upon his shoulder, and he could hold them back no more.

In a halting voice that strengthened as she continued, she began to recite the Twenty-third Psalm. " 'The Lord is my shepherd; I shall not want. He maketh me to lie down in green pastures. . . . Yea, though I walk through the valley of the shadow of death, I will fear no evil. . . . and I will dwell in the house of the Lord for ever.' "

With the words, the pain faded from her face. Only the certainty of her faith remained.

How beautiful she is, Peter thought, *how serene in her conviction.*

"I'm tired now. I think I'll sleep." But she continued to grasp Jacob's hand, unwilling yet to release him.

As Peter turned, she looked up at him and, for just an instant, he saw reflected in her gaze the strength and determination that had defined her. She gestured him close and whispered into his ear, "Take care of our Becca."

⁂

After the funeral, Peter gripped Becca's hand as she stood, stoic and unsmiling, beside her father, enduring the repeated condolences of the mourners.

"I can get through this," she muttered to Peter. "For Papa's sake."

In the days that followed, much as he tried to, she would not be consoled. She remained sequestered in her room, leaving it only at mealtimes.

One evening, as Helga began clearing away the supper dishes, Becca remained at the table, staring morosely into space and absently toying with the uneaten food on her plate.

Across from her, Peter put his elbows on the table and rested his chin on his clasped hands, watching her. Finally, he said, "It's time you let your anger go, Becca."

She pushed away her plate. "You're right. But if I have to hear one more person tell me it's God's will, I think I'll scream." She said it just as her father walked into the kitchen with a book of poetry that he'd brought from his library.

She sucked in her breath. "I didn't mean for you to hear that, Papa."

Jacob's gaze was tender. "You don't have to worry about my feelings, Becca girl. I'll survive this." He smiled at Peter. "As we all will."

Becca's eyes teared. "If I'd had to listen to another religious platitude, I might not."

"They mean well." Her father patted her shoulder.

" 'She's gone to a better place,' " Becca intoned and grimaced. "And with such assurance, as if they'd seen it for themselves."

"That's what your mother believed," Peter murmured.

"Well I don't." Becca turned on him fiercely. "Not anymore. And I don't believe 'time will heal,' either." A sob burst from her. "I'll always miss her. What do they know? Platitudes.

That's all they are. Meaningless platitudes."

"It sometimes seems that way." Her father sighed. Sinking into his chair across from Faith's rocker, he turned his face to the fire.

Peter gazed at the rocker, imagining Faith sitting, rocking, absently humming a favorite hymn as she stitched. Now and then glancing up to bestow a smile on one of them.

He longed to hear her voice and see her smile. He even longed for one of her small sermons or discourses on life. He smiled to himself. That just showed how much he missed her. . .loved her.

He sat, his elbow on the table, his cheek resting on his fist, following Jacob's gaze into the crackling fire, its light dancing off the pine walls and the silent family. Behind him, dishes clattered as Helga dried and put away the plates from supper.

"I've been doing a lot of thinking, Becca." Jacob turned toward his daughter and reached out his hand, an invitation for her to come and sit on the floor at his feet, as she'd done since childhood when her dog, Max—long gone—had curled up next to her.

Becca took a lingering breath and rose. Dropping down beside him, calmed, resting her head against his knee. For the moment, the fight was out of her although, Peter knew, not the anger.

Pensive, they stared into the fire.

Jacob broke the silence. "I reckon age has a lot to do with our perspective on death." Absently he patted Becca's shoulder. "Whether or not we believe death is an interruption or an end."

"Don't," Becca interrupted, bitterness evident in her voice. "All I know is, I'll never see Mama again. I call that an end."

Ignoring her anger, Jacob continued. "In the Bible, Jesus demonstrates that God sees it differently," he said. "God views death as a two-sided coin, life and death connected." He frowned, considering, measuring his words. "The space between our coming out of the womb and our dying, this is our space in the world that is seen. Most of death is at the end, beyond our sight." He looked down at her. "Do you understand what I'm trying to say, Becca?"

"Oh, dearest Papa, you sound as preachy as Mama." She smiled, hoping to lessen the sting of her bitterness.

Jacob chuckled.

A moment of his old self.

"You're probably right, Becca girl. After almost twenty-five years, the woman taught me well, for sure." His expression grew tender as his thoughts drifted. He looked down again at his daughter. "We all go through grief in our lives, Becca. More than once if we live long enough. But it needn't be so overwhelming if we can see it as an absence, not a loss."

He looked over at Peter. "Son, in Faith's Bible, see if you can find the passages in Second Samuel about the death of King David's son. I think it's around chapter 11—12—one of those."

"Knowing Mama, she probably has it underlined," Becca muttered under her breath.

Peter got up, went over, and picked up the Bible from the table beside Faith's chair. It took him a few minutes. "You were right. It's chapter 12. Verses 16 through 23."

"Sit down and read it to us." Jacob nodded to the rocker.

Peter could see Becca tense. He would be the first to sit there since her mother's death. He sat then looked up and was comforted by Jacob's nod to begin.

" 'David therefore besought God for the child; and David fasted, and went in, and lay all night upon the earth. And the elders of his house arose, and went to him, to raise him up from the earth: but he would not, neither did he eat bread with them. And it came to pass on the seventh day, that the child died. And the servants of David feared to tell him that the child was dead: for they said, Behold, while the child was yet alive, we spake unto him, and he would not hearken unto our voice: how will he then vex himself, if we tell him that the child is dead? But when

David saw that his servants whispered, David perceived that the child was dead: therefore David said unto his servants, Is the child dead? And they said, He is dead. Then David arose from the earth, and washed, and anointed himself, and changed his apparel, and came into the house of the Lord, and worshipped: then he came to his own house; and when he required, they set bread before him, and he did eat. Then said his servants unto him, What thing is this that thou hast done? thou didst fast and weep for the child, while it was alive; but when the child was dead, thou didst rise and eat bread. And he said, While the child was yet alive, I fasted and wept: for I said, Who can tell whether God will be gracious to me, that the child may live? But now he is dead, wherefore should I fast? can I bring him back again? I shall go to him, but he shall not return to me.'"

When Peter had finished, they sat silent, the sacred words seeping into their hearts.

Finally, Jacob said, "Death's a cold, hard reality, Becca. Just remember, Jesus reminds us that life continues even when the body stops. The Gospel message is that we don't have to hold tightly, even when our hearts are broken, even when we're crying over the absence of someone we love. There is still a future." He reached for her hand. "Just remember all things come together in God's time."

But from the look on Becca's face, Peter wasn't sure she was willing to wait, if she even believed it all. The realization weighted him down. There was more to mourn than the loss of their beloved mother and friend.

seven

In the last month, Becca had thought a lot about what Papa had said about death. It had had a familiar ring. Very familiar. One way or another it had been drilled into her since birth that the body was merely a house for the soul, that there was life after death, that all things came in God's time, etcetera, etcetera. It was all so familiar, in fact, that long ago she'd given up paying attention.

Until now.

But then, "now" was the first time she'd had to deal directly with the reality of death.

Her grandparents on Papa's side and Mama's father had all died before Becca was born. Grandma Wilcox died after that, but she was far away and very old and Becca hardly knew her.

Now at eighteen she was having to come to terms, and it wasn't easy, even when she accepted—more or less—those lessons her father now preached. She'd even come to realize that, though time didn't heal all, it did heal some and certainly helped to ease the pain.

Still, there were moments, least expected, when she would see Mama's face, hear her voice—especially in terms of conscience—smelling the scent of roses or biscuits in the oven—and remember with such vivid recollection that tears flowed before she even realized it. She supposed time would take care of that, as well. But not entirely. And that was as it should be. Those moments of remembering, even if they brought tears, were precious.

Life went on.

It was a morning in late June. Becca and Peter hooked old Henry up to the buckboard for their weekly trek into town to purchase supplies and to pick up the mail. Afterward they were having lunch with Jane, as they often did.

Since graduation, Jane had been living with her father in the sheriff's cottage next to the jail. "I'd deputize her if she wasn't a girl," her widowed daddy often said, and with good reason. Not only did Jane keep house for him, she kept the jail spotless and cooked for the incarcerated men—which amounted largely to random rustlers and weekend revelers. It was rumored that her imaginative meals were good enough to do time for. . .which may have accounted for the number of repeat offenders.

It was noon by the time Becca and Peter pulled into town. The street was almost deserted at that hour, except for a buggy parked beside the bank across the way and a horse tethered to the rail in front of the blacksmith's shop next door. Peter waved at Farmer Apple's teen boys leaning against the rail outside Thompson's General Store on the far side of the post office. He jumped from the buckboard and came around to help Becca down, but already her feet had hit the plank sidewalk, her gingham skirt swinging.

At the sound of their boots clacking across the scuffed wood floor of the deserted post office, Henrietta Pryce glanced up from her lunch with the expression of one annoyed by an inappropriate intrusion. Rising impatiently, she stepped over to the counter and reached under it. "A package for you, Becca," she said in her quick, precise way. "From Ohio. . .your dear departed mother's sister."

The small, wood-framed building also housed the telephone office. The Pryce sisters, Henrietta and Hazel, had been Whispering Bluff's postmistress and telephone operator, respectively, since the town got a separate building that would also house the newfangled telephone operators. They were tiny, gray-haired women with beaked noses, prominent ears, and beady, knowing eyes. They reminded Becca of hummingbirds with their sharp, fast movements and their spiky, assertive natures. They looked almost identical in their blue-striped smocks, although Henrietta was a tad taller and Hazel a year older. Together they kept the community informed. What one knew, the other told. . .and vice versa.

Henrietta handed the package to Becca. "A new dress, no doubt, judging from the box."

I'm surprised you didn't tell me the color, Henrietta.

"Aren't you going to open it?"

"Thanks, I think I'll wait 'til later."

Obviously disappointed, if not slightly miffed, the middle-aged postmistress turned, pulled a stack of letters from the slot marked *H*, and began thumbing through them, separating a bundle from the middle of the pack. "Looks like seven letters this week. . .and a refund check"— she turned the envelope over—"from the Garner Feed Company."

For how much? Becca restrained herself from asking, though she was sure the busybody knew.

Henrietta handed the letters to Peter. "There's one more here. . . . It's addressed to a Hostettler, but nobody I've ever heard of—"

Becca's heart leaped.

"I almost returned it to the sender but thought I'd wait and ask you folks. In case it was a relative."

"What's the name?" Peter asked.

"R. Wilcox. . . R. Wilcox Hostettler."

Becca rubbed her damp hands on her skirt, her heart pounding.

Finally!

Peter frowned. "I don't know an R. Wilcox Hostettler. Do you, Becca?"

She snatched the letter from Henrietta's hand. "You know very well it's for me, Henrietta." She hadn't missed the shrewd look in the woman's eyes. "If you didn't, it would be a first." She turned and strode out of the post office, the letter clutched in her hand, the package under her arm.

Peter jogged behind her. "Becca—"

"Wilcox is Mama's maiden name. You know that."

"Oh yeah. I forgot. But why—"

She tossed the package into the back of the buckboard. "I thought I might have better luck getting accepted at the university if they didn't know I was a girl." As she spoke, she tore open the envelope and began to read. When she'd finished, she stared down at the sheet and then into space. "With all that's happened, the accident, Mama dying, I don't even care anymore."

"Oh, Becca, I'm so sorry." Gently Peter took the letter. After the salutation he read, " 'As Dean of Admissions, I am pleased to inform you that. . .'"

He looked at Becca in shock. Then he grinned. "You've been accepted, Becca. You've been *accepted*."

He pulled her into a bear hug, lifting her off her feet. Whooping and laughing, he spun her in circles, his boots kicking up pebbles in the dusty street.

"Put me down!" Becca cried, struggling with one hand to keep on her straw hat, with the other pounding ineffectually against his chest. "You're making a spectacle of yourself."

"This is a spectacle-making moment."

"Peter, put me down this instant!" she shrieked, her hat slipping awkwardly off her head.

The blacksmith's head popped out of his shop.

"Now who's making the spectacle?" Peter laughed, ignoring her protests.

Luke Thompson limped out of Thompson's General Store. He leaned on his crutch. "You young 'uns." He shook his head and retreated back inside.

The Apple brothers, in front, leaned against the rail, laughed, slapped their thighs, and mimicked in squeaky voices, "Put me down, Peter. Put me down, you naughty boy."

Henrietta and Hazel Pryce stood side by side in the doorway of the post office, their hands folded in front of them, their mouths pursed in disapproval. "I told you that was what the letter was about," Henrietta declared. At which point Hazel turned, no doubt to spread the news on the party line.

"If you don't put me down—"

And finally he did, quite unceremoniously, right there in the middle of the street.

Furious, Becca picked up her fallen hat and dusted if off. She was giving him a piece of her mind when Jane ran across the street, blond curls bouncing, flounced skirt bobbing about her dainty ankles.

"Hush, or I'll have you both arrested for making a public nuisance." She grinned at them. "And I'm the girl who can do it. What's going on?"

"Search me." Peter shook his head, obviously perplexed. "I thought Becca'd be the one excited. Turns out it's me."

"About what?"

Becca slapped her hat back on her head. "It doesn't matter. I'm not going anyway."

"You're not going?" Peter roared.

"Will you two quiet down? Not that you've much of an audience. . ." Jane looked both ways down the empty street and caught sight of the gawking Apple brothers and Henrietta. "They don't count," she said in a voice that carried.

She grabbed Becca's and Peter's arms. "I think we can find a more suitable place to discuss this—whatever it is. You can tell me all about it over lunch."

In a tiny plot behind the jail, Jane had created a paradise of perennials, roses, and blooming lilac, sweet-smelling herbs and garden vegetables. Beneath the shade of a spreading chestnut in a corner of the garden, on a round table covered with lace, she had arranged goblets and the china Becca's mother had given her. In the center of the table stood a mixed bouquet.

"Mama would have been proud of you," Becca mused. "You're everything she wished for in a daughter."

"As are you," Jane said staunchly, giving her a hug. "Two sides of a coin, we are." She spread her arms. "Now how can you two argue in such a setting?" She turned to Peter. "You're a good sport to put up with a lady's fancies; but not to worry, I've made us man-sized roast beef sandwiches and potato salad, and there's fresh peaches." She took a breath. "And lemon tarts. Your favorite." She smiled up at him.

"Why don't *you* treat me so good?" He gave Becca a conciliatory grin.

"Because I'm not sweet on you like Jane is," Becca replied with a toss of her head.

"Oh please." Jane's blush betrayed how close Becca was to the truth. A suspicion she'd held for quite some time.

"You two sit down," Jane commanded. "All I have to do is put ice in the lemonade."

Sheepishly Becca and Peter complied, but the minute Jane disappeared inside, Peter exploded again.

"Becca, I can't believe you!"

"Well, do." She glared at him. "Besides, it's my business, not yours."

"It's never been that way before. We've always confided in each other. Now you throw this at me."

She pulled the pins out of her straw hat and dropped it on the grass beside her. "All right. I decided after Mama died, but I was afraid to tell you."

Peter leaned forward, the peacock chair squeaking beneath his weight. "Faith wanted you to go to the university."

"Mama wanted me to go to finishing school."

"You know she changed her mind about that." He clamped his mouth shut, assessing Becca through narrowed eyes. Slowly he said, "I think you're using that as an excuse. I think you're afraid. I think for all your bluster and grand intentions, now that it comes right down to it, you're scared. Scared for the first time in your life that you might fail."

"How dare you say that, Peter." Becca leaped to her feet. "What do you know about it?"

"I know you. Better than anybody, Becca," he said quietly. "I see it in your eyes. And I'm here to tell you that you won't fail. You can't. It's not in you."

Becca plopped back down into the chair. "All right. So I'm afraid; who wouldn't be—going away from home for the first time into a sea of strangers who don't want you there in the first place. But it's not failing that I'm afraid of. I know I can make it. What frightens me is my lack of passion." She looked down at her clasped hands. "I love animals; you know that. But when a human being dies, like Mama did, because there's no doctor near enough to help, somehow taking care of animals doesn't seem that important to me anymore."

Peter reached across the table, his dark eyes warm with compassion. "What is it you *do* want, Becca?"

"I don't know," she said miserably. "All I know is what I don't want. I no longer want to be an animal doctor."

He withdrew his hand, sat back in his chair, and crossed his arms. "Could it be that my dulcet girl—my sweet girl—wants to be a human doctor?"

Oh, he could read her mind, that brother of hers, and discern the secret thoughts she'd been too sorrowful to admit, even to herself.

Becca didn't answer.

"Aha!"

"Some chance I'd have."

"But R. Wilcox Hostettler might."

Jane came down the back steps bearing a tray laden with their picnic fare. Peter, ever the gentleman, hopped up to help her.

"So?" she said, pouring lemonade from a frosted pitcher.

"Becca got accepted to the university." Peter reached for a sandwich.

"How wonderful!" Jane turned toward her friend. "But I'm not surprised. Not one little bit. I always knew you would make it."

"She says she's not going."

"You're not going?" Jane cried. "But why?" She put down the pitcher.

Peter gave Becca a sidelong glance. "She doesn't want to leave her papa and me." He took a large bite of sandwich, chewing appreciatively.

"The ego of some people." Becca arched a brow and took a sip of lemonade.

"That's ridiculous. They're grown men, Becca; they can take care of themselves. And Helga comes six days a week. Besides, Daddy and I are always here. . .if they need us."

Her fond glance at Peter was not lost on Becca.

"Oh, Becca." Jane's large, lavender eyes were damp. "You're so special. You always have been. It's not that you're just smart and accomplished; there's a fire in you. You're different from Peter and me. We're content to stay here and make our lives in Whispering Bluff."

Becca had been noticing for quite some time how often Jane linked her name with Peter's. She was so guileless and open. Becca couldn't understand why Peter didn't see it.

"Say you'll think about it, Becca, so we can all enjoy lunch."

"I'll think about it."

"Then I have no doubt you'll do the right thing," she said, obviously relieved. "You've always been a very sensible girl." She picked up her napkin. "Have you two finished your shopping?"

"We got as far as the post office." Peter reached for another sandwich.

"You must look at the new fabrics Mr. Thompson just got in, Becca. There's a lovely polished blue cotton that would look just beautiful on you, and I saw a Butterick pattern that would be perfect for a traveling costume."

"I'm not much of a seamstress, Jane." Not that Becca cared about clothes, anyway.

"But I am." Jane patted her hand. "Now that Faith is gone, your wardrobe is up to me." She rubbed her dainty hands together. "I can hardly wait."

To get me out of the way.

Becca shot a glance to the oblivious Peter. For a smart fellow, he could certainly be dense sometimes.

❧

For the last mile home, the buckboard rattled along between

the Osage orange hedges that separated the rutted road from the fields. It was midafternoon, and the warm air was rich with the earthy smell of alfalfa and fresh-tilled soil.

Peter broke their silence. "You know, I'm going to miss you, dulcet girl."

"I haven't said I'm going, yet."

He smiled at her. "You will."

"You're so sure."

He didn't answer.

His certainty irritated her. "If I do go to the university, I have no worry about your being lonely. You always have the Singleton twins."

He made a face.

"And Jane."

"Don't be ridiculous," Peter growled.

"That's not so ridiculous. Jane's sweet on you, Peter. I'm sure of it. And if I wasn't before, I am now, the way she looked at you today."

"She looks at all the boys that way."

"She does not!" Becca said, incensed. "The Singleton twins, maybe, but not Jane. You'd have to be blind not to see it."

"Did you ever think I might not *want* to see it? I'm fond of Jane, for sure. But not in that way."

"Another little sister?" Becca leaned against him, looked up in mock adoration, batting her lashes.

He shrugged her away. "That's enough, Becca," he said sharply.

"Oh, for heaven's sake, Peter. Can't you take a joke?"

He looked down at her, his dark eyes strangely serious.

"What?"

"Nothing."

And then he was himself again, snapping the reins and urging old Henry into a trot.

But the moment had lasted long enough to make Becca notice.

eight

R. Wilcox Hostettler
Box 33
Whispering Bluff, Colorado

*It is my pleasure to inform you that your request to transfer
your application to the school of medicine has been approved.
Registration is on Friday, September 3, 1898, between
9 a.m. and 3:30 p.m. in Fullrider Hall. Classes commence
the following Monday, September 6.*

Yours very truly,
Hector Dodd, Ph.D.
Dean of Admissions

And so it was that Becca found herself on that final day in
August 1898, looking out the train window as it moved slowly
away from the platform at Whispering Bluff. Never had a
train whistle sounded so mournful. Never had Papa and Peter
looked so dear, as they stood side by side, waving good-bye.
She watched until in the distance their two figures merged
into one and all that was left was a smudge on the spinning
landscape of golden fields beneath a blue sky. And the plaintive
whistle of the departing train.

It was an overnight trip from Whispering Bluff in Sedgwick
County to Denver and a long wait to catch the spur to Boulder,
plenty of time to regret that she'd been so adamant in refusing
Papa's and Peter's offers to accompany her. "If I'm smart enough
to be accepted into medical school, I'm certainly smart enough
to get there," she'd insisted. But as the miles clacked along, she
realized their presence would have had less to do with her being
smart and more to do with love. Already she missed them.

She remembered other trips: to Silver Springs to see the circus when she was nine. The train was as exciting as the circus. That was the year before Peter arrived. Then there was the trip to Denver when she and Peter had qualified for the finals of the state spelling bee. The whole family had spent a week there. After the competition, they'd gone to the zoo and the botanical garden. She'd gotten lost in the botanical garden, but she hadn't been afraid. She'd known her family would find her.

But now she was on her own, without the security of their presence. If she floundered, they would not be there to rescue her.

But God is.

She heard her mother's voice as clear as if she were sitting next to her, repeating the first lines of Psalm 27: " *'The Lord is my light and my salvation; whom shall I fear? the Lord is the strength of my life; of whom shall I be afraid?'* " She found herself mouthing the words as she watched the green fields of alfalfa slide past.

Somehow comforted, her spirits began to lift, and by the time the white-jacketed waiter strode down the aisle, announcing dinner, she was beginning to feel the first pangs of hunger. Papa had paid extra for her meals in the dining car. No eating at stops along the way for his girl.

Swaying in the doorway of the dining car, Becca paused to scan the elegantly appointed space with its linen cloths, crystal goblets, small vases of fresh flowers. . .and the rowdy foursome—young men of approximately her age—seated nearby. Defying their bold glances and murmured asides, she sailed past, following the waiter to a table for two near the rear of the car, already occupied by a robust, gray-haired matron in a plumed hat, her nose in a book. The woman did not lift her gaze, but the unblinking glass eyes of a stone martin stole slung round her shoulders never left Becca. Still, Becca's appetite was not deterred as she consumed a delicious dinner of antelope steak, corn on the cob, and fresh fruit.

&

Later, zipped into her upper berth, she was soon lulled to sleep by the monotonous sway and sound of the moving train and slept soundly until morning. Waffles in the dining car and then back to her seat, excitement mounting as she watched the changing landscape. Gone were the vast plains. In their stead, she could see the grandeur of the Rockies as the train snaked through the mountains. More trees, more shanties along the tracks, more people waving, more stops exchanging passengers; and then the hustle and flow of the Denver station, where she had time to stretch her legs and caught sight of the same raucous rogues at the far end of the platform, playfully harassing some other pretty prey.

She dared not stray far from the coach. What if the train took off without her? Becca smiled to herself. *Well, so much for the brave, confident girl who insisted, "I can do it myself, Papa."*

Then, at the brief stop just before Boulder, she disembarked at her destination.

R. Wilcox Hostettler had arrived. A shiver, more fear than thrill, rolled down her spine.

She was not alone. Others, clearly students—men—poured out from the coach behind in raucous disarray, slinging their luggage and stumbling over each other.

Among them was the ubiquitous foursome. The tallest spotted Becca, gave a low whistle, and strolled toward her.

She looked down, busying herself with the pair of satchels at her feet.

"Well, here you are again, sweet girl."

She swung around.

Sweet girl. . .dulcet girl. Peter's silly pet name for her.

She wasn't sure which upset her more, the reminder of Peter and home or the young man's audacity.

Silently she glared at him, chin high, arms akimbo, aware of the leering bunch egging him on. Daring him.

"Whoa." He stepped back, palms upraised. "Just trying to be friendly."

"Or show off in front of your chums." She glanced at the group behind him.

"My profound apologies." He bowed and backed away.

He was handsome. A blond, athletic, collegiate sort. And *tall*.

Maybe I shouldn't have been so prickly.

But she was saved from further rumination—or regret—by the appearance of a stooped black man with a grizzled beard and hair twigging from beneath a moss green jockey cap that matched his striped shirt. As he approached her, his thumb twanged the right suspender that held up his neatly pressed black-and-white-checked knickers.

He bowed slightly and removed his cap. "Miss Becca Hostettler?" he inquired in a gravelly voice.

She nodded.

The only girl on the platform.

"Mrs. Gotts sent me."

"Wonderful. My trunk is in the baggage car."

&

The ad for Mrs. Gotts's Boardinghouse ("Only respectable guests need apply") that Papa spotted in his weekly copy of *The Denver Post* had turned out to be just the beginning of a long and embarrassing process. First he'd had Jane's daddy check with a fellow sheriff in the university town to be sure that Mrs. Gotts's was a legitimate operation and not a house of ill repute in disguise.

"With a name like Gotts? Please, Papa, you've got to be kidding."

Still, he was not wholly satisfied, and numerous pieces of correspondence between him and Mrs. Gotts had followed. And then, much to Becca's chagrin, there was a long-distance telephone call with additional questions.

A father couldn't be too careful.

Becca was sure her future landlady would expect some overprotected, spoiled, hothouse flower, incapable of taking care of herself. To say nothing of the fact that now all of

Whispering Bluff would know the particulars of Becca's itinerary and accommodations at the university—via the Pryce sisters' gossip network.

Nevertheless, here she stood at the foot of the wooden steps leading up to the yellow Queen Anne–style house with its gabled roof and odd-shaped windows, and beside the entrance was a white sign with crisp blue letters: MRS. GOTTS'S BOARDINGHOUSE.

On the porch above her waited a tall, lean woman, her brown hair pulled back in a tight, efficient knot. She wore a blue and white gingham dress and a bemused expression as she clasped her hands over her starched apron.

"Rebecca Hostettler, I presume."

"Mrs. Gotts?"

The woman nodded.

"Please call me Becca." Adjusting her straw sailor hat, Becca lifted the skirt of her navy cotton dress as she climbed the steps. "I hope my father's concern for my well-being didn't cause you too much trouble." She had reached the top and stood face-to-face with the raw-boned, pleasant-looking woman who was less intimidating up close than she had been from below. "Believe me, I'm far more capable of taking care of myself than he'd like you to believe. You know how fathers are."

Mrs. Gotts lifted her hand. "Indeed I do. I have three grown children of my own. I remember how my dear, departed husband used to try to protect our only daughter." Mrs. Gotts smiled.

Becca decided she was going to like this lady, with whom she saw eye to eye. Literally.

Mrs. Gotts called down to the conveyance, "Radd, please take Miss Becca's things to the corner bedroom upstairs on the right."

"Yes'm, Miz Gotts." The wiry old man lifted Becca's satchels as if they held feathers and bounded up the steps, brushing past them and through the screen door, allowing it to slam behind him.

Mrs. Gotts rolled her eyes at the sound she'd obviously never gotten used to.

The wooden floor of the wide veranda was painted yellow to match the walls of the house, but the newel posts and rail matched the white trim of the windows, as did the eight rockers facing the street, four on each side of the front door.

"The one on the end is yours." Mrs. Gotts nodded to the right. "Dare not by mistake sit yourself in anyone else's. Folks are very proprietary of their space."

"I'll certainly be careful," Becca assured her, speculating on the disposition of her fellow guests as she followed the landlady into a large parlor with its wood-burning stove, blue upholstered couches, and brightly braided rug. To the right, a round Victorian game table with four spindle-back armchairs stood in the middle of the book-lined alcove where a small writing desk and chair were tucked beneath the octagonal window. A cheery room, indeed!

"I suppose you're ready for lunch," Mrs. Gotts said. "We eat in fifteen minutes. You'll have the opportunity to meet some of the guests. Breakfast is served at seven, lunch at twelve thirty, and dinner at six forty-five, precisely." She reclasped her hands. "I expect everyone to be on time. If by chance you are too tardy to be served because of your classes, you may help yourself in the kitchen to whatever is left over." She moved toward the stairs to the left of the alcove. "Baths are scheduled on Saturday mornings, beginning at seven thirty."

From her cadence, it was obvious that Mrs. Gotts had repeated this precise litany many times.

"I'll show you your room. Give you time to wash up," she said as they ascended. "There are four guest rooms on the Maple Street side. The three across the hall from them overlook the back garden."

Mrs. Gotts paused at the landing where the stairs divided, half going up to the second floor. She inclined her head toward the half descending to the back porch. "To the ordinary—the privy. Do you need—"

"I can wait, thank you."

"My room is on the right," she continued, reaching the top of the stairs and turning to the left down the narrow hall. "Although all our guests pay the same, you have one of the more desirable corner rooms with a view of both the back garden and Fullrider Avenue."

"That sounds lovely."

"As your father requested." Mrs. Gotts smiled indulgently as she unlocked the door and handed Becca the key.

When they entered, Becca could see that her satchels and trunk were already beside the tall pine armoire with its double doors. At the end of the narrow room, under a round window, there was just enough space for a bed and small night table next to it, and in the left corner was the washstand and a chamber pot on the lower shelf. There was a corner window to the right of the bed; under the window on Becca's right sat a small desk and mismatched ladder-back chair with a cushioned seat.

Hardly the spacious, artistically appointed bedroom she was used to, but with its polished pine floor, blue-painted walls with the white-trimmed windows and ceiling, and the matching blue and white muslin coverlet and curtains, it was a happy room, and Becca's spirits lifted with relief.

Mrs. Gotts had even placed a vase of daisies on the bedside table.

"I like it," Becca said, turning to her new landlady. "I like it very much."

Mrs. Gotts looked pleased.

"Everything's so cheerful," Becca said, feeling more was expected, "and clean."

"It's up to you to keep it that way. The only thing Radd does is empty the chamber pot in the morning." She glanced at her watch. "Lunch at twelve thirty. You have ten minutes."

nine

Ten minutes!

She could unpack later.

Becca tossed her hat and gloves onto the bed and made for the door. She hurried down the hall and hurtled down the steps into the backyard.

It had been a long morning.

As she approached the ordinary, she stood back in surprise.

A two-story privy?

She'd never seen one in Whispering Bluff. A door above with no stairs?

She heard a chuckle behind her and turned to see Radd leaning on a rake under the elm, his eyes twinkling.

"You'll git it in the winter when the snow's ta the eves."

Of course. When drifts of snow covered the lower door, the second level could be used without the need to shovel a path.

The summer and winter castle!

She laughed, closing the door behind her.

She hadn't had to attend university classes to learn something new, she thought, hurrying back toward the house a few minutes later.

There were three at the oval table for eight: a round, distinguished-looking gentleman in his midseventies, with muttonchop whiskers, twinkling blue eyes beneath bushy eyebrows, and a monocle dangling on a gold chain from his checkered vest, who Mrs. Gotts introduced as Colonel Higby; Lulu Perkins, across from the chair Mrs. Gotts had designated for Becca; and Mrs. Gotts herself, presiding at the head of the table, her back to the kitchen.

Spooning the fragrant vegetable soup into the bowls Radd had placed in front of her, Mrs. Gotts said, "Lulu is a gifted seamstress and milliner." She cast a smile at the stylish, brown-haired woman. "I fear we'll be losing her soon if her gentleman friend has his way."

Miss Perkins blushed, placing a thick slice of fresh-baked bread on her plate and passing the basket to Colonel Higby.

"He'll be getting a jewel, that he will," the colonel blared, as the hard of hearing do.

Mrs. Gotts continued. "Miss Tattler is our local librarian. She takes her lunch to the library, and of course Grace Preen eats with the children at the elementary school where she teaches. She's just a bit older than you, Becca. You'll meet them both at dinner." She handed Becca a bowl of soup to pass on to Colonel Higby. "Harrison Wilkie, our writer, takes most of his meals in his room, and the Fortiers are rarely here because they're preparing for the opening of their new French supper club." She handed Becca a steaming bowl then served herself.

Becca lifted a spoonful of carrots and celery in a savory-smelling broth, allowed it to cool, and took a sip. "This is delicious."

"The vegetables are from Radd's garden." Mrs. Gotts gave him an appreciative smile as he cleared away the empty tureen. She helped herself to a wedge of bread, spreading it with a thick slather of butter from the crock in front of her, took a healthy bite, chewed, and swallowed. "Becca will be registering for medical school tomorrow," she said, in a voice meant to carry to Colonel Higby.

"Oh?" Lulu Perkins looked surprised.

Becca smiled indulgently, used to that reaction.

"Medical school?" Colonel Higby boomed. "That's like Mrs. Gotts joining the French Brigade." He laughed and slapped his knee. "Good luck, Miss Hostettler, you're gonna need it, sure as h—"

"Colonel!" Mrs. Gotts gave him a sharp look. "Don't pay him any mind," she said softly aside to Becca. "The colonel's of another generation."

Not many years beyond your own, Becca thought. Mrs. Gotts was a very forward-thinking woman. No wonder she was so drawn to her new landlady.

After lunch, it didn't take Becca long to unpack and set out on a tour of exploration. As she breathed the clear, crisp air of mile-high Boulder, she reflected on how different it was from the little rural town of Whispering Bluff, with Boulder's tree-lined avenues, foothills thick with foliage backing up to jagged mountain slopes, and the river rushing through the middle of town, bringing the mountain coolness. *Oh, the coolness!* How welcome that was at this time of year.

It was midafternoon when she strolled by the new university hospital, due to be completed in November, according to the brochure she had received. Standing on the northeast corner of the campus, on the crest of a hill overlooking Boulder Creek, the hospital was a boxlike structure with long windows and a steepled roof. Thirty beds, so the brochure said. *Imagine, that many!* And the most modern equipment. Someday she'd be an intern there, in a white jacket, stethoscope flying.

She laughed. She wasn't even registered and was already dreaming of being an intern.

There were other students, some wandering like her, others hurrying along with purposeful strides. But she paid little heed, imagining herself bending over a microscope in the laboratory in Medical Hall, the two-story brick structure nearby that looked more like a mansion than a medical school with its wide veranda and dormer windows.

So while she yearned for home and those she loved, she was also filled with anticipation for a whole new world that was about to open up for her.

❧

The next morning, however, standing alone at the edge of the quad—the only woman in sight—she did not feel nearly so positive as she tried to ignore the grins and whistles of the brash young men rushing around her, their blazers bright in the morning sun, their neckties flying.

She felt like a guppy in a sea of sharks.

"The Lord is my light and my salvation; whom shall I fear? the Lord is the strength of my life; of whom shall I be afraid?"

Thank you, Mama, for reminding me!

She adjusted the folder under her arm, straightened the tie of her gray-striped Gibson girl blouse, smoothed her skirt, and gave the top of her straw boater a resounding smack.

She wasn't her mama's daughter for nothing!

She took a deep, protracted breath and headed for Fullrider Hall.

She didn't need a map to find it. The Gothic structure was the most imposing on the Boulder campus, with its cupolas and spires, gables and turrets, its stacked windows blinking in the sunlight.

"I declare. Miss Nose-in-the-Air."

At the sound of the taunting baritone, Becca found herself staring up into the grinning face of the audacious young man from the railroad station.

"What are you doing here?" He cocked his head, giving her just enough time to collect herself.

"The same thing you are, I imagine." She brushed past him.

He caught up, keeping stride. "Obviously, you're new."

"How can you tell?" The chill in her voice didn't deter him.

"You're heading toward the medical school."

"Thank you for your help." She started up the wide steps.

"The nursing school is on the other side of the campus."

"I'm aware of that."

"Well, then where are you going?" He bounded ahead and planted himself in front of her, beneath the columned portico, barring her way. "Surely you're not enrolled in the medical school."

"Why not?" She glared at him, trying to pass. But he refused to budge.

"But you're a girl."

"How astute of you. Can you direct me to the registrar's office?"

The look of surprise on his lean, aristocratic face could not have given her more satisfaction. But with a blink, it dissolved again into his expression of mocking humor.

"The first door on your right. There's a sign that reads REGISTRAR'S OFFICE. You can't miss it."

She sailed past.

"Aren't you going to say, 'Thank you'?"

"Thank you." She pushed open the heavy oak door.

"Good luck!" She heard him chuckling as the door swung closed behind her.

Three young men filling out forms at the counter looked up as Becca entered the office. Behind the counter stood a middle-aged clerk with a collar so tight it made her severely coiffed head look like the cork on a bottle of seltzer. She paused from sorting a stack of papers and glanced up. "Yes?"

"I'm here to register."

The woman returned to her task. "The nursing school is—"

"On the other side of the campus," Becca interrupted. "I know. I'm here to register for medical school." She heard a snicker and looked over to see the young men exchanging glances of amusement.

The clerk put down the sheet she was holding. "I'm afraid there's some mistake."

"I don't think so." Becca laid her folder on the counter, drew out her letter of acceptance, and handed it to the clerk.

Lips pursed, the woman studied it through her small, thick glasses, frowned, and pointed an accusing finger at the salutation. "This letter is addressed to an R. Wilcox Hostettler."

"I am R. Wilcox Hostettler."

She peered at Becca more closely, her tone suspicious. "That's a man's name."

Becca gave her a tight smile. "The *R* is for 'Rebecca.' Rebecca Wilcox Hostettler. There was nothing on the application that indicated women need not apply. And, as you can see, I have been accepted."

"This is highly unusual. I'm afraid I can't act on this without speaking to the dean."

A snort from the shortest young man made it clear where his sympathies lay. Becca glared at him and saw by the exchanged looks that the other two were in full agreement.

Dunderheads!

Frustration and embarrassment fueled her fury. So maybe she had been accepted under false pretenses. She'd met the requirements. More than met them, she'd exceeded them. She willed herself to remain calm. "I would like to speak to the dean, personally."

"He's in a meeting."

"I will wait."

"He won't be back until this afternoon." The clerk crossed her arms, lowering her head and glaring defiantly over her glasses. She clearly wasn't about to let some little whippersnapper get the best of her.

Becca stared back. "At what time will he return?"

"One thirty. But—"

"I will be here at one thirty," Becca pronounced. "Promptly."

"Suit yourself." The clerk got back to the business of sorting. "But I wouldn't hold out much hope if I were you. There's a precedent, you know."

Smug old biddy!

"What precedent is that? That gender overrides intellect and academic performance?"

At the sound of clapping behind her, Becca whirled around. The office door stood ajar, held open by a man's booted foot.

Becca almost pushed him over as she stormed out.

"Whoa. Wait a minute. I'm on your side."

"I'll believe that when Pike's Peak is covered by the ocean," she muttered.

He barred her path as he had earlier.

"Get out of my way!" She danced side to side, trying to pass him, and he did likewise, just as determined not to let her.

"Come on. Just give me a chance."

In the instant that it occurred to her that he might just be sincere, he had taken her arm and led her away from the door to the corner of the foyer, positioning himself to prevent her escape.

"Look. I heard what went on in there, Rebecca Wilcox Hostettler, and I thought you were splendid. I have two sisters of my own, and I'd be proud if either one of them showed even half of your grit and courage."

My goodness. He seems to mean it.

Blocked by his imposing frame, Becca realized that her first impression of the young man's good looks had been accurate. . . maybe even underappreciated. A broad-brimmed boater tilted rakishly on golden curls, beneath which his devilish blue eyes twinkled. He had a smiling, generous mouth and a slightly crooked nose that kept his face just this side of perfection. His blue blazer, stylish on the other lads, hung elegantly from his broad shoulders. A matching tie, knotted at his stiff round collar, was tucked neatly into an impeccably tailored plaid vest.

And he was *tall*.

And, at the moment, he was not a bit audacious. Rather, he looked very kind and quite comforting in his commiseration.

She leaned back against the wall and lowered her gaze. "Thank you. I appreciate that."

"You're welcome." He stood looking down at her, quietly assessing. "You know, Rebecca—"

"My friends call me Becca." She gave him a grudging smile.

"Becca. I have an idea that might help you out."

"Who says I'll need help?"

"What do you think?" He waited.

She slumped deeper against the wall.

"Well?"

What did he have in mind? What would he expect in return for his favor—if indeed he could produce one? Was it worth the risk?

Then it occurred to her that perhaps she was being a bit egocentric to question his motives. After all, she was a farm girl from Whispering Bluff, not a peep-show siren.

She glanced up. He still looked sympathetic.

"Let me at least try. . . . Of course if I do something for you, you have to do something for me."

Aha!

"I hope you'll let me take you to supper." He looked very sweet when he asked, almost shy.

"You don't have to bargain."

"You mean you would dine with me anyway?"

She couldn't help but smile. "I didn't say that."

His teasing grin returned. He straightened. "I'd like to chat, but I have work to do. I'll meet you back here at one thirty." At the door he paused. "*Promptly,*" he added, in a mimic of her admonition to the clerk, and grinned.

"Wait!" Becca called. "I don't know your name."

But the door had already swung closed.

ten

September 1898

On the third evening after Becca left, Peter leaned against the newel post of the front porch in brooding silence, while Jacob, in the porch swing, placidly sanded the whistle he'd just finished whittling.

Only three days and it seemed as if she'd been gone forever.

His gaze wandered down toward the barn and silo, the paddock, the windmill and the well, the tiny village of sheds and outhouses, muted silhouettes in the moonlit landscape. Absently his eyes followed the pale ribbon of road to where it disappeared at the crest, then reappeared only to be lost again in the inky, star-studded horizon.

Without Becca to share it, it was an empty landscape, missing the essence of its splendor.

He'd known he would miss her, but never in a million years could he have imagined how much.

He and Jacob had stood on the rickety platform of that pitiful little shanty they called a train station and waved good-bye to Becca. As he'd watched the train disappear around the bend and heard that last, long, lonely whistle, his heart had lurched with a desolation that hit him with the impact of an avalanche.

Just as the family had begun to adjust to a life without Faith, when there'd been fewer days of mourning and more of joy, Becca had left.

Now he realized how much of that joy depended on her.

He missed her teasing laugh and her quirky sense of humor, the way she caught the gist of his jokes, and how she always knew the right things to say. . .and said them with such ease and candor. He missed their passionate arguments about—well, just about anything, from God to what to bring to the church picnic. He missed sitting next to her on the porch steps at dusk as the shadows lengthened, lulled by the rustle of leaves in the elm, the crickets' chorus, and the creak of the porch swing.

He missed doing the chores with her in the early morning when the dew was still damp on the grass and sitting next to her on the bluff at sunset, sharing confidences and dreams.

He missed her tangle of auburn hair. He missed her gray eyes, warm and soft as a mourning dove's throat when she was sad or sleepy or, when she was angry, cold as the winter ice on the Rikums' pond. He longed for her strong, lithe body striding beside him, the scent of spring lilacs that suffused the air when she sat next to him on the buckboard on their way to town.

The house, the rustling leaves, the crickets were the same as when she'd left, the porch swing now creaking under Jacob's weight as he wordlessly rocked back and forth. But for Peter, the house was a shell, quiet and lifeless without her life within it. The rustling leaves, the crickets, a rude cacophony. Even the creak of the porch swing was a desolate reminder.

And she'd only been gone three days!

A faint whinny drifted from the barn. Fireflies darted among the shadowed rhododendron clustered at the base of the oak.

Jacob cleared his throat. "Ran into Widow Jensen at Thompson's store this morning. She says she's ready to sell her land, now that Victor's gone, move east to be with her daughter. She asked if I was interested."

"Hmm." Peter was listening with half an ear, locked in his loneliness.

"I told her I didn't think so." Jacob momentarily stilled the swing as he reached over to put the sandpaper on the wicker side table next to him and picked up a cloth. "I'm content with things as they are." He proceeded to polish the wood with even, methodical strokes. "I'm not getting any younger, and with Faith gone. . . Even if we didn't farm the land ourselves, I have enough income from our tenants and from my investments to live comfortably the rest of my life." He ran his fingers over the whistle's smooth surface. "There's plenty of work around here just keeping up with our livestock and the orchards, the garden. . .and my books, to keep me happy." He leaned back in the swing and began to rock again. "Then I got to thinking. About you. . .and Becca."

Becca and me?

That got Peter's attention. He turned.

"So I told her I'd consider it, but I needed to talk it over with you first."

A small flame flickered in Peter's heart.

"Since you and Becca will eventually be owning the farm."

His breath caught. "I didn't know that I would—"

The porch swing stopped abruptly. "I assumed you understood that." Jacob's voice had a tone of puzzlement.

"Well, I guess. . ." Peter hoisted himself off the steps. "I guess I figured I'd be running the p–place." He took a deep breath and repeated more slowly, "Running the place for Becca. With her being a doctor and all."

The swing creaked as Jacob leaned forward. "You love this land, Peter; it's where you belong. And it needs to belong to you."

Peter sank back against the porch rail. "I. . .can't—"

"What do you mean, you can't?"

"I can't believe it."

Jacob laughed. "There's no one I'd want to have it but you, and there's no one I'd trust but you to take care of my Becca."

"That goes without saying," he said softly.

"Yes."

From Jacob's quiet response, Peter sensed Jacob had surmised things that he himself was just now allowing himself to admit.

"I don't know what to say."

"You don't have to say anything."

"You've always been so good to me, so generous. Treated me like a son."

"I've only treated you the way I feel. You've been a son and more; you've been a friend, a compatriot. Someone I could talk to who shared my interests." Jacob chuckled. "You know how rare that is in these parts. . . . And you love my daughter as much as I do."

Even more!

Jacob rose. He stood for a moment in silence. Quietly he said, "My only regret is that Faith and I didn't adopt you when you were young. But the years went along, and it all seemed so natural that we didn't think about it." His voice thickened with emotion. "We didn't think about it from your standpoint."

Peter tried to swallow. He blinked back the unmanly moisture that had sprung to his eyes. "It–it's not what's on a piece of paper, Uncle Jacob; it's how a person is treated that makes him feel like a. . .a son."

Jacob put his arm across Peter's shoulders. The light was too dim to make out Jacob's expression, but the depth of feeling in his next words was clear. "Faith believed, as I do, that God intended you for us, Peter. And you've been such a blessing"—his voice cracked—"far greater than we possibly could have imagined. Far greater than you'll ever know."

Peter was too moved to speak. Even if he'd been able, what words could possible convey the deep love and gratitude he had for this family who had taken into its home and hearts a small, skinny, lost soul with a sad past and little hope for the future, and made him its own?

Jacob pulled out his handkerchief and blew his nose. "Enough of this. An old man needs his sleep. Tomorrow we'll put this inheritance thing on paper. Make it legal." He moved toward the door. "And talk about that Jensen property while we're at it." He pulled open the screen door. "You coming?"

"You go ahead. I'll be up in a bit."

"All right then. Good night."

"Good night."

No way could Peter sleep. Too much roiled inside him. He needed to sort it out. He walked down the path toward the orchard.

He had always wanted Becca to live her dream, encouraged her. That she'd been accepted into medical school made him as proud and happy for her as if it had happened to him. But he hadn't counted on how bereft he would feel. Or how her absence would magnify the insecurity he felt for his own future. He had known where he wanted to be and what he wanted to do, but how it was all to be accomplished was as hazy as the morning mist.

Until tonight!

He turned and trudged slowly up to the crest of the hill. He lowered himself onto the cool grass, feeling its spikes against his palm, smelling its freshness, hearing the whisper of a soft breeze playing across it.

For sure, this came as close to heaven as earth could provide.

He wrapped his arms around his legs and rested his chin on his knees, gazing out at a horizon canopied with stars. Someday this would be his land and Becca's. He would make it the finest in the whole valley. He'd make use of what he'd been reading in the *Farmers' Almanac* and the various periodicals about new, innovative techniques of production and land use and more efficient methods of crop rotation. He'd make Hostettler Farm the best example of efficient farm planning and operation in the county.

Becca would be living her dream, he would be living his, and with time, their two dreams would become one.

She would come home to the valley a doctor; they would get married and have children. He would see to it that she had the best medical equipment available, a strong horse, and a fine carriage so she'd be safe when she made her medical rounds. But he'd never let her go alone at night or in inclement weather. He would be there to keep her safe. . .and to carry her medical bag, he laughed, if she'd let him.

Jacob had offered him the fulfillment of a dream he hadn't been bold enough to imagine. He would work the land he loved in the most beautiful spot on earth; he would have the woman he loved. . .and children, lots of children to fill the house with laughter.

What more could any man ask for?

He looked back toward the house. A light flickered in an upstairs window and went out.

"Thank you, Uncle Jacob. . .and Aunt Faith," he whispered.

eleven

Becca leaned against the wall in the hall outside the registrar's office and followed the hand circling the face of her new wristwatch. One twenty-five.

"Promptly," the audacious young man had said—how else could she think of him but audacious? She didn't know his name.

He had five minutes.

In the past, she had never spent much time ruminating over members of the opposite sex. She'd had her share of beaux in Whispering Bluff, usually sweeter on her than she on them. The few who did attract her were either too short, a prejudice of which she was not proud, or, if tall, already snared by some simpering sweetie with more looks than brains. This had not made her particularly unhappy since she preferred horseback riding with Peter anyway. Basically she'd been content in his company and that of Papa, surrounded by the peace and beauty of her life on the farm.

But now she had thrust herself into a new life with new and exciting surroundings and possibilities and the heady attention of a dashing young man—and other leering lotharios. The attention both confounded and secretly pleased her, even though she had to attribute much of it to lack of other female competition. She wondered if her fellow medical students would change their tune—and their smiles—when they found out they had to sit next to her in class.

She glanced at her watch again. One twenty-nine. . .and he was nowhere in sight.

So much for my knight in shining armor.

She was nominally disappointed but not unduly surprised, given his carefree charm.

Her Peter would never have treated a lady that way. If he'd promised, he'd be there. And on time!

She pushed open the door to the registrar's office. Different male students from before—but with the same smirking curiosity—looked up from the forms they were filling out. The same pinched-faced clerk greeted her with an affronted glare and glanced at the clock above the door as if she were peeved by Becca's punctuality. "The dean is expecting you," she said brusquely.

"Thank you." Becca swallowed a smart retort and sailed past her into the dean's private office.

Behind the massive mahogany desk, Dean Dodd eyed her with cold assessment.

He did not smile.

Everything about him was dark: his eyes, his slicked-back hair, his sparse, defined mustache; black bow tie against a stiff white collar, black jacket and vest, unrelieved even by the glint of a gold watch chain.

Her heart sank.

He looked like an undertaker, one quite capable of delivering a eulogy on her unmourned demise at the university's school of medicine.

The desk was empty of papers except for one single sheet upon which his pale hands were tightly folded.

"Be seated." His nasal voice had an asthmatic twang.

Mustering all her courage, she returned his scrutiny with a pleasant but unflinching gaze as she lowered herself into the chair opposite him, her folder in her lap.

Without preamble he began. "This application is a fraud!"

"I beg your pardon?"

"In my opinion, R."—he paused—"*Wilcox* Hostettler, you applied for admission under false pretenses."

Her pulse accelerated. "That is my name, sir."

"Clearly"—his arrogant gaze scanned her from the top of her straw sailor hat to the white-gloved hands in her lap—"you are not a Wilcox."

"The application is quite accurate, Dean Dodd. Wilcox is my middle name, after that of my mother's family. My first name is Rebecca. . .hence R. Wilcox Hostettler."

"Be that as it may, your intention to mislead the committee is obvious."

"That assumes, sir, that there was any need to mislead." The blood pounded in her temples. She lifted her chin. "As I pointed out to your clerk, there is nothing on the application that precludes women from applying."

The dean's face flushed. "I don't appreciate your tone, Miss Hostettler; it will not help your cause."

"I apologize, Dean Dodd, if I sounded—what shall I say— intense? I assure you it is merely because I feel so keenly about the integrity of my application."

"So you say." His eyes narrowed. "That aside. . .it is my opinion that you should *not* be admitted to our medical school."

His attitude since she'd entered his office had served as a warning, and yet she sat mute, her mouth agape.

How could it be? Surely she hadn't come all this way to have her dreams dashed in a single sentence. By an *opinion*! It was outrageous!

And yet, hadn't she once admitted to Peter that "just in case" she had applied as R. Wilcox Hostettler?

Still, she'd read the fine print so carefully—no mention of gender on the application, no photograph required, just a stellar academic record. And that she had provided.

She felt hope draining away. What could she do? What could she say to persuade him?

But the withering resolve in the man's pallid, contemptuous face let her know it would do no good to argue. Begging would only give him satisfaction.

But she could not be defeated. She balled her hands into fists.

"Whom shall I fear? the Lord is the strength of my life; of whom shall I be afraid?"

This was not the end. She would find another way. She started to rise.

"Unfortunately, I am governed by a higher authority, our board of trustees."

Shifting the responsibility. As if he has no culpability.

"It seems the matter of your admission has rather mysteriously been referred to them, and they. . .the chairman of our board, to be precise, has ruled that since your application was not technically fraudulent, and you were formally accepted, the university has no choice but to admit you."

What?

Were her ears deceiving her? Did he just say what she thought he said?

She slowly lowered herself back into her chair, staring at him in disbelief.

His expression of petulant anger and injured pride said it all. His authority had been usurped. The decision on which he had taken such a resolute and passionate stand, in the end, had been overruled, and he was humiliated.

He had known from the start of this meeting that she had been accepted. But he had played it out just the same. She could only surmise he'd done so out of meanness and to feed his own squashed ego.

Relief washed over her.

It didn't matter.

She might have even felt pity for him had she not realized that he was not through with her yet.

"I feel it my duty to offer a word of caution," he continued. "Trust me, you will not be welcomed here, Miss Hostettler. And I intend, personally, to see to it that your conduct is closely monitored."

Becca gripped the folder in her lap.

Unbelievable!

The man seemed intent on adding insult to injury.

As if I were some hussy conniving to corrupt the innocents within these hallowed halls.

Judging from what she'd already observed of their blatant ogling and lascivious remarks, they'd already been corrupted.

"I appreciate your warning," she said steadily, not about to let her sharp tongue give him the excuse he wanted to dismiss her.

"Furthermore, do not expect special treatment because you are a woman."

"I would never—"

His sharp stare stilled her interjection. "On the contrary, if you are to remain in this medical school, you will exhibit the highest level of performance."

"I always try to do my best," she murmured, still gripping the folder.

"Hopefully, for your sake, it will be good enough. And finally, you are not to form a distraction by mingling with the other students but will be provided an assigned seat at the back of the hall. You will not participate in discussions, and you will take your tests separately." He handed Becca a single sheet. "Give this to the clerk. She has been instructed to register you for classes beginning Monday." With that he swiveled his chair around, busying himself with a stack of papers on the credenza behind him.

Becca had been dismissed.

She chose the counter in the far corner of the registrar's office to fill out the required forms, her back to the room, as far away from the inquisitive eyes and mocking comments as she could get.

How naive she had been, how unprepared. Yet she hadn't been too naive; she was here, after all.

Nevertheless, the weight she had expected to lift lay heavy. Her goal to return one day to Whispering Bluff and provide the medical services that might have saved her mother's life had a new set of obstacles. The isolation and disdain she faced would be arduous and lonely.

In this room of vaulted ceilings and hostile strangers, she longed for the familiarity of home: of blue skies and prairie grasses, of Papa by the fire and Peter's comforting arm around her. Especially she longed for Peter, who understood her better than she understood herself, who had the uncanny knack of knowing the right words to lift her spirits. Peter, her advocate, her friend, her brother, the rock on which she leaned. Peter: the rock. He was well named.

She ignored the jocular murmurs and mocking asides from her fellow students as she handed the clerk the forms to be processed. It seemed that they'd heard about her admission and were bent on making her life as miserable as possible.

If she had been the teary sort, now would be the time. But she was not. Quite the opposite! Rather than defeat her, their rude behavior would only serve to strengthen her resolve.

From the day she was born, equality and justice had been ingrained in her and, above all, faith. Even had she wished, she could not separate herself from what she believed.

A strength—*"which passeth all understanding"*—welled within her.

She slid the schedule of classes into her folder and tucked it under her arm. Glancing neither to the right nor to the left, with the regal bearing of her resolve, she strode past the line of male students and out the door.

twelve

There he stood, in the hall outside the registrar's office, the audacious one, legs apart, hands in his pockets, bowler tilted jauntily on the back of his curly head.

"How did it go?"

No excuse for not being prompt? "Not exactly as I had expected."

"I'm not surprised, considering you were dealing with Dean Dud." His look held wry compassion. "He's of the old school."

"So I discovered."

She should be upset with him for not showing up when he said he would. But here he was now, and he seemed genuinely interested.

"As it turned out, it didn't matter that you weren't here. Assuming that you could have helped, I didn't need it."

He leaned back against the pillar. "So you did it on your own. Congratulations!"

"Well, not exactly. It seems that mine is a unique case—"

"We knew that."

"Which they sent to the board of trustees for review. In fact, it was the chairman of the board who made the final decision."

He grinned. "Dr. Fullrider."

She nodded. "I must say I congratulate him on being a forward thinker. Unlike the dean of admissions."

"Unfortunately, the dean's view is shared by too many at the university." He pushed open the double doors to the portico and ushered her ahead of him. "I hope the fact that I didn't make it back before your meeting won't discourage you from having supper with me to celebrate." His beguiling smile was far too confident for his own good.

"I never promised I would, and even if I had," she said

primly, "we haven't been properly introduced."

"Then may I introduce myself," he said, with a half bow. "My name is Winston."

"I'm not sure that will do, Mr. Winston—"

"Winston is my first name."

"Oh?" She cocked her head and waited.

"If I tell you my last, you won't hold it against me?"

Becca couldn't help but laugh. "With a name like Hostettler, how could I?"

"It's. . ." he mumbled.

"Yes?"

"It's Fullrider," he blurted. "Winston Fullrider."

"Fullrider? As in Dr. Fullrider?"

He nodded.

"As in Fullrider of Fullrider Hall and Fullrider Avenue and the mansion on top of Fullrider Hill?"

"My grandfather." He looked embarrassed.

Becca stood, nonplussed. She didn't know what to think or say—but only momentarily. "You ran off earlier because you were going to talk to your grandfather?"

He shrugged.

She should be grateful. Instead, she found herself annoyed. "Why didn't you tell me?"

"Would you have, in my place?"

"I'd like to think so." She sighed. "Well, maybe not."

"To be honest, I didn't know how he'd react. He's very conservative, as you can imagine. However, I'm happy to say, he responded as I'd hoped." His smile was smug. "Especially when I pointed out the legal ramifications."

"Legal ramifications?"

"I advised him that the university had represented to the applicant R. Wilcox Hostettler—her true name—that she had been accepted; that in reliance on that representation, said R. Wilcox Hostettler had expended considerable time, effort, and money, and that undoubtedly, she had a meritorious cause of action in the event that the university failed to honor its commitment. In other words, you could sue. You would have, wouldn't you?" He grinned.

"Of course! Indeed." By this time, Becca was choking with laughter. "You sound more like a lawyer than a doctor."

"I am. I'm graduating from law school next June."

At that moment, a dark-haired, athletic-looking lad in an outfit similar to Winston's punched him on the shoulder as he ran past. "Hi, Winnie."

"Winnie?" Becca giggled.

"One of the brothers. I'll take care of him later."

"Well, Mr. Fullrider—"

"Winston."

"Not Winnie?" She couldn't resist.

He frowned.

Answer enough.

"Well." She gave him a sidelong smile. "I suppose you're who you say you are."

"Is that a yes for supper?"

"When did you have in mind?"

"Is tonight too soon?"

"I'll have to inform my landlady so she won't prepare for me."

"Where are you staying?"

"Mrs. Gotts's Boardinghouse."

"On the corner of Main and Fullrider." He grinned. "Very respectable."

"Tell that to the dean."

Winston quirked a brow.

"He told me my conduct would be closely monitored. Apparently he's concerned I might lead his young innocents astray."

"Oh yes, indeed. You do look like a dangerous woman." Winston laughed. "I can only hope."

❧

He took her to a little supper club tucked between elegant shops on a street with sidewalks in the upper part of town.

In the middle of the intimate room, a crystal chandelier

cast prisms of light on the peach brocade walls and matching cloths, the array of goblets and silver, the tea candles, and the fresh flowers that adorned each table.

Becca had once read in a romance novel that peach was the color most flattering to a woman.

It must be true, she thought as she surveyed the stylishly elegant ladies in their silks and satins, glittering jewels and feather boas, the ostrich plumes adorning their upswept hair.

Fingering her mama's locket, she glanced down at her modest gray dress with its fitted waist and draped bodice. She felt like a dandelion that had suddenly sprouted in a hothouse full of exotic flowers.

Had she lost her mind? Why had she said yes? What could a simple girl from Whispering Bluff possibly have in common with the scion of Boulder society?

But here she was, gazing across the table at Prince Winston, with his tawny curls gilded by candlelight, his blue eyes glittering, his athletic build adorned by an elegant high-winged collar and bow tie, high-button waistcoat, and cutaway jacket.

It was enough to turn a girl's head. . .to make a girl's breath catch. . .more than once.

The murmur of conversation punctuated by ladies' laughter and gentlemen's rich baritones, the clink of cutlery and crystal, the harmony of violins, the scent of savory food drifted like a soft breeze around them.

Winston leaned across the table. "I'm definitely with the prettiest girl in the room," he said, covering her hand with his.

Is he mocking me? Primly she withdrew her hand. "Then you either need glasses, or I'm forced to doubt your veracity."

"I resent that."

"I'm sorry," she said, glancing at the sophisticated matrons at the adjoining tables. "But I do recommend you have your eyes checked." She lifted her chin, feeling some spunk return. "That is not to say I am without my merits."

"Modesty among them." He laughed.

"False modesty is a false virtue. I know who I am, as clearly, so do you."

"That's one for you! But I still refuse to be deterred, Miss Becca Hostettler. If I may, before I was so rudely interrupted: I find large intelligent eyes streaked with silver quite beautiful. I find a generous mouth that smiles easily, enchanting. I find skin as smooth as tawny silk, of unmatched beauty—"

"Oh, *please*." Becca rolled her eyes.

"I'm just about finished. And. . .I find unruly auburn hair especially beautiful."

"How can you say that?" she exclaimed, patting her attempt at a neat bun.

"I'm referring to these wisps that refuse to be tamed." He reached across the table, lifting a recalcitrant curl from her nape. "And if you think I've rehearsed this speech, you're right. I've been rehearsing it since the moment I set eyes on you at the train station." He leaned forward. "And for your information, Miss R. Wilcox Hostettler, you are a very intimidating young woman. I find you a challenge that I want to meet."

"That's a compliment?"

"Simply a fact."

"Winnie, is that you?"

Winston did not wince at the sound of his hated nickname. "Emily?" He jumped to his feet, a welcoming smile on his face. "I had no idea you were home."

"Only briefly. I'm leaving tomorrow for New York to visit Auntie Laurel for a week. And then back to Paris."

The young woman was about Becca's age, but there the similarity ended. She was blond and petite with delicate bones and soulful blue eyes and a soft, almost breathy quality to her voice, which ended each sentence on an up note, as if she were asking a question.

"So soon?" Winston looked disappointed. "I had no idea you were coming home. If I'd known—"

"When you didn't write, I didn't think you cared," she

murmured, her lids fluttering down to her décolletage. Absently she toyed with the silk flower at the diminutive waist of her pink, brushed-silk gown.

"Of course I cared." His voice was hardy with assurance. Suddenly he remembered Becca. "Oh, I am sorry! May I introduce Miss van Pelt. Emily, my friend, Miss Hostettler."

My friend, he had inserted. But to which of the two had he wished to make that clear?

With languid grace, Emily van Pelt extended her gloved hand. "Any friend of Winnie's is a friend of mine. Call me Emily."

"Call me Becca, Emily."

"We're celebrating Becca's acceptance into medical school," Winston said.

"Oh my." Emily raised her eyebrows as she lifted her hand to her bosom, as if it was all too overwhelming to believe. "I am impressed."

Becca shrugged modestly. "Being accepted is one thing. Graduating is another."

"But a woman in medical school." Emily turned to Winston. "Your friend must be quite brilliant. Not just some little ol' artist like me." She blinked twice.

"Little ol' artist, pshaw!" He turned to Becca. "This young lady has already had an exhibit in Paris."

"In Paris. Congratulations." Becca refrained from mimicking, "Oh my" and fanning herself as if it was all too impressive to believe.

"Just a creaky little gallery on the West Bank."

"Still—"

"Emily's one of my sister Anna's best friends."

Emily smiled. "And yours, I hope."

"That goes without saying."

"Well, I must be off. The Clarks will be waiting. We're going to see *The Importance of Being Earnest* at the Biloxi. I hear it's a very good performance. Lovely to meet you, Becca. Good luck in medical school." She put her hand on Winston's arm. "This time you write, hear?" She got up on her tip-toes and brushed his cheek with a kiss, pirouetted, and floated between the tables until she'd disappeared into the foyer, Winston's gaze following her every dainty step.

Almost reluctantly, it seemed to Becca, he sat back down and spread the napkin across his lap.

So why did she care? She didn't really. She didn't know him well enough to care. But she noticed.

Men can be so naive. Even sophisticated, worldly ones like Winston.

"Emily's like a sister."

"I could see that."

He doesn't see the irony.

"We grew up together. Emily was always at our house or Anna at hers." He looked up at the white-jacketed waiter standing patiently by the table. "Yes, Chandler?"

"An aperitif before dinner, Mr. Fullrider?"

"Becca?"

"No, thank you."

"I'll get the wine list, sir."

"None for me, thank you," Becca said.

"You don't even drink wine, Becca?"

She shook her head.

"I can see I have a rich opportunity to expand your education beyond the classroom."

"I don't think so."

"Is that so?" Winston chuckled. "My teetotaling grandmother would approve of you, Becca girl." He looked up at the waiter. "We'll pass on wine tonight, Chandler. Just the menu."

As the waiter removed the wine goblets from the table, Winston said, "I'm curious. Why?"

"For not drinking?"

He nodded. "Is it personal or for moral or religious reasons?"

"I would think personal would include the other two."

"I suppose." He thought for a moment. "Then you don't judge other people?"

"That's up to the Almighty."

"I'll drink to that." He lifted his glass of water. "And now a toast. To Dr. R. Wilcox Hostettler: Long may she be a woman of her convictions."

thirteen

September 4, 1898

Dear Papa and Peter,

Well, it's Saturday, and I can say that I am registered in medical school. . .but not welcomed. In fact, it was nip and tuck. The dean of admissions asserted, possibly with some merit, that I had been accepted under false pretenses. Anyway, my case was taken to a "higher court" and reversed by the chairman of the board of trustees, who just happens to be the grandfather of my new friend, Winston Fullrider.

In celebration, Winston invited me out to an elegant supper club. I would have felt quite out of my element had he not been so charming and nice. It doesn't hurt to have friends in high places. . .even if only one. I hope it lasts.

You would like Mrs. Gotts, Papa. She is a very forward-thinking, no-nonsense lady, and, I suspect, she will keep as sharp an eye on me as you would hope. Much to my regret! (smile)

I met Lulu Perkins and Colonel Higby at lunch my first day, and this morning at breakfast, I got acquainted with more of my fellow guests, all who were here, that is, but the elusive writer, Harrison Wilkie. Although he may have been the shadow I passed coming back from the privy last night.

There is a volatile young French couple who live across the hall (and keep no secrets); and Miss Tattler, a tiny, twitchy, mouselike librarian who, I declare, has the musky smell of the stacks.

And then there's Grace Preen. She's an elementary school teacher, about my age. Mrs. Gotts said she thought we'd be chums, and she was right. Grace is blond, plump, and pretty (but not as pretty as our Jane) and likes to read and take walks and talk, talk, talk, just like I do.

Mrs. Gotts sets the tone for a warm, family atmosphere, and it seems to work. And thank goodness for that. I doubt I'll have many friends on campus with whom to commiserate. Except, of course, Winston, but he's a senior in law school and far more serious than he seems, so I'm sure his nose will be to the grindstone, as will mine.

I can't begin to tell you how much I miss you both. I miss watching you whittle, Papa, and reading the Bible in front of the fire, and Helga's good cooking—although I can't complain about Mrs. Gotts's fare. I miss our long walks, Peter, sitting on the hill at dusk and watching the stars come out, one by one; smelling the grass and listening to the katydids; and our long conversations when we solve the world's problems.

Nevertheless, I feel you're all with me, in my heart. As is Mama, whose hymns still hum in my ear and whose quotes from the Bible ring clear in her beloved voice, lifting my lagging spirits and reminding me of the source of my strength (although I am still having some issues with the Almighty.)

Anyway, I love you all, kisses all around—that includes Helga.

> *Your beloved daughter and sister,*
> *Becca*

P.S. Peter, I'm dropping off a note to Jane, but when classes start, I doubt I'll have much time, so I'm counting on you to keep her up-to-date.

> *XXOO*

P.P.S. Classes begin Monday. Keep me in your prayers!

❧

September 9, 1898

Dear Papa and Peter,
Today was the fourth day of classes. I didn't write before because I hoped things would get better, and I didn't want

to sound like a whiner and worry you with something you couldn't do anything about.

The very first day, the dean addressed the class by declaring my presence, saying, "We have to accept this woman; she has gotten the best of us. The board of the university decided in her favor." This announcement was greeted with catcalls and clapping, rude comments and leering glances by my fellow students, which the dean did little to subdue.

Had I been of weaker fiber, I easily could have burst into tears. As it was, I did not let my steely gaze move from the blackboard behind him. (When I related it all later to Winston, he was appalled and was ready to take up arms and report the blackguard to his grandfather, which I opposed at once. I need no more of Dean Dodd's hostility than has already been heaped upon me.)

In the amphitheater where lectures are given, I have been relegated to the back (where the air is thin, needless to say) in an assigned seat as far away from the lecturer and other students as possible. Fortunately, I inherited your keen hearing, Papa, and Mama's keen eyesight, or I would have no hope.

Already we have had two short quizzes on the material, which I am required to take in another room. My assignments are not passed to the front with the other students but must be handed in separately.

But that is not the end of it. When I'm not jeered, I'm shunned, passed on campus as if I were a pariah. (Now I know how the Shulamites in ancient Israel felt. A bit of hyperbole, but I am that miserable.)

Oh, the injustice of it. I feel like a sacrificial lamb!

How did those first women doctors back East and overseas survive this kind of treatment? What grit they must have had! I read about one woman in England, Dr. Miranda Barry, who spent her life disguised as a man. They didn't discover it until after she died. (That is one sacrifice I am not prepared to make.)

But when I hear stories such as that, it strengthens my resolve. It's almost as if I have an obligation to continue the battle. (Does that sound like a drumroll?)

Maybe it is. And maybe it's the stubborn spirit I inherited from Mama, an inner resolve that I'm not going to let them get the best of me. My goal to become a doctor is more important than my poor, neglected ego.

I will show those supercilious males that women are as smart—maybe smarter—than they are. It will give me great pleasure to wipe off their smirks and silence their rude remarks. From now on, they will have to race to keep up with me!

Already I feel better.

Your beloved daughter and sister,
Becca

P.S. On a more positive note, you'll be happy to know I found a church in the neighborhood. It looks very much like our church back home with its Gothic styling and arched window above the entry. The simple cross in front above the choir loft makes me feel at home. Mama would approve. The sermons are good but lack the fervor of Pastor David's.

XXOO

❧

December 12, 1898

Dear Papa and Peter,

It has been over three months since I started medical school. It hardly seems possible. I'm pretty much taken for granted now, ignored rather than ridiculed, and even have a friend or two. I guess the rest of the "supercilious males" have gotten the message that I'm not going away. (It probably didn't hurt that Winston came to class one day and sat next to me, glaring at the offenders. He can be very intimidating when he wants to be.)

I still have to wait on the men to finish with the research materials before I am allowed access and rely on my friend Bradley Klinker when I need to use a microscope.

My notebooks are filled with drawings and descriptions of diseases and terms like clavicle, scapula, sternocleidomastoid, and acute gastroenteritis (the common stomachache). Are you impressed?

My classes in chemistry, toxicology, and physiology are now making sense. (Anatomy has made sense all along.) Next year, my confusion will begin again with therapeutics and obstetrics. But I LOVE it. If I ever had doubts about becoming a doctor, I don't any longer.

I continue to be at the top of my class, making the men rush to keep up, as I vowed. Hopefully they are becoming enlightened to the fact that medicine is a science dependent on brains and skill, not brawn or gender. Hopefully!

I can't even talk about Christmas. Even when I think about it, my eyes tear up. I miss the smell of pines and the glisten and crunch of the snow on our evening walks. Not that there aren't pines. I have forests and snow up to my knees—but too much, too deep, and not the same as that great sweep of sparkling white against the crystal blue sky that we get in the plains.

I know you would have been willing, Papa, but I couldn't allow you to spend more money so soon just to bring me home, only to send me back practically on the next train.

Mrs. Gotts has decorated in a gaudy, Christmas way, quite out of character for her but bright and festive, and each of us has added a personal touch. I made a wreath from pine branches and attached pinecones and apples and nuts and tied it with a wide red ribbon, the way Mama always did. Everyone made a big to-do about it when Mrs. Gotts hung it on the front door. But I cried.

My own room I decorated with a few leftover pine branches and a red ceramic bowl Mrs. Gotts lent me. I filled it with apples and walnuts and branches of holly and put it on my desk. Not quite what I'm used to, but at least it smells like the holidays.

Two more Christmases and I'll be home for good.

Did you get my presents? I hope you like them. I included Jane's in the package so I wouldn't have to send a separate parcel.

See those wet splotches on the paper? They're my tears.

I miss you. I miss Mama.

Love,
your devoted daughter and sister,
Becca

❧

December 26, 1898

Dear Becca,

I can't pretend it's been a "merry" Christmas. Without you here to share it, how could it be?

Uncle Jacob and I were hardly in the mood this year to string popcorn and cranberries, cut out snowflakes, or bake gingerbread boys to trim the Christmas tree. That was your job. . .and Aunt Faith's. Ours was to hang them.

We did cut a tree, though. Saved the spindly little specimen from succumbing to the wind and gave it a dignified demise. Out of pity, Helga swept up the dried needles and tied red bows on its limp branches.

We put Aunt Faith's porcelain crèche on the mantel, though I doubt she would have approved the placement. You know how finicky she was about the exact spot for Baby Jesus. He had to be just so.

I laid out the Nativity Uncle Jacob carved. I remember there were only Mary, Joseph, and Baby Jesus when I came. The second year I was here, he added the three wise men. . .or was it the angel? Anyway, now the whole Christmas pageant's spread out beneath the tree.

Lots of snow, but no snowball fights, no sliding down the

*hill on the double sled with you clinging to me, screaming as
we barely miss the oak. Your cold nose, warm breath against
my cheek. A tradition I hold dear. The clinging, not the
screaming!*

Church Christmas Eve. Last year, there were the four of us.

*We had Christmas dinner at Jane and the sheriff's. She
really put herself out, as you'd expect, but the turkey wasn't
up to Aunt Faith's. I don't think your mama put the recipe in
writing, but hopefully it's a genetic pass-down. Someday I
want to taste it again. Does that sound like a hint? It is!*

*Incidentally, Jane loved the scarf and matching mittens
that you sent her. Pink, her favorite color! Good choice!*

*And thank you for my leather gloves. They're great, and
they fit perfectly. How did you know my size? I especially like
that outer stitching. I wear them every day. There must be
fine stores in Boulder. I've certainly never seen anything to
equal them on the shelves at Thompson's G. S.*

*As for the fancy new penknife you sent Uncle Jacob, it's
hardly been out of his hands since he opened the package. By
next Christmas, no doubt, he'll have whittled at least a dozen
more creatures for Noah's ark.*

*Well, I guess it's time to close. The fire's beginning to flicker,
and Uncle Jacob's already gone to bed.*

*Thanks for all the presents, but please understand when
I tell you that your papa and I would trade them all for a
glimpse of you. Next year, if I have to come to Boulder and
carry you back personally, it'll be Christmas in Whispering
Bluff for you, dulcet girl. . . . (Hey, I oughtta write a song.)*

*Behave yourself, Becca, and don't forget those back home
who love you.*

Peter

fourteen

A warm chinook wind had melted much of the snow, leaving dirty gray piles against the wood-frame buildings and muddy tracks down the main street of Whispering Bluff.

In front of the post office, old Henry's tail twitched, but his drooping head didn't lift as Peter tossed the package of shirts Uncle Jacob had ordered from the Sears & Roebuck catalog into the back of the buckboard. Peter hopped up into the seat and dropped three of the four letters into the satchel beside him; then he impatiently yanked off his fur-lined gloves, stuffed them into the pocket of his Pendleton jacket, and tore open the one addressed to him. Unfolding the single page, he read:

December 26, 1898

Dear Peter,

I don't have time right now to write a real letter, but I couldn't wait another minute to at least let you know how deeply grateful I am for your wonderful, wonderful present.

My own microscope! I can't believe it! You can't even begin to know how thrilled I am. And a Zeiss! How could you possibly afford it? How did you know? I just don't have enough words or paper (or time at the moment) to thank you enough.

Oh dear—they're calling me from downstairs. I have to go; Winston's waiting to take me to the library. Would you believe I have an assignment due the day after New Year's, and I'm only halfway finished? Luckily it's in anatomy, my best subject.

So for the moment, you must read past the brief words to what's in my heart and know how grateful I am. It's a gift I will treasure all the rest of my life and never forget who gave it to me.

Thank you, thank you, thank you, my precious brother. More later.

Your loving sis, B.

Precious brother! Loving sis!

The words cut like a knife.

He slapped the sheet on his knee.

Would she never think of him as anything other than her brother?

His heart that had stepped up pace at the sight of her letter now fell to a ponderous slowness. He breathed a dejected sigh. Why would he expect her to feel differently? What had he ever said to make her believe otherwise? Absently he gazed at the sheet in his hand. He hadn't even realized the depths of his feelings himself.

Hardly an hour passed that she wasn't in his thoughts.

He'd been counting on Christmas to tell her how he felt.

Practicing was more like it! And then to find out she wasn't coming home. What a blow!

And then, to top it all off, when he was hoping, praying that her heart would grow fonder in absence, this Winston kept rearing his ugly head.

Before it went any further, he had to write to her.

No, what he had to say couldn't be written in a letter; it had to be said face-to-face.

But there wasn't time to wait.

But what if she didn't take him seriously. . .or was affronted by his audacity. . .or worse, what if she took pity on him for his pathetic passion?

Dejected, he folded the letter and returned it to the envelope.

Surely God meant them to be together. It would be too cruel

a joke if this desire, this need for Becca's love that dwelled in his heart with such certainty, such intensity, was not sanctioned by the Almighty.

"Yoo-hoo, Peter."

Oh no! Jane!

He was in no mood for her cheery chatter.

She came tiptoeing across the muddy street, skirting pot-holes, her arms extended like balancing wings in her gray, fur-lined cape.

"I hoped you might be coming, seeing as it's postal delivery day." She skipped over a rut. "Just in case, I made those ginger cookies you love so much."

She'd almost reached him when her little booted foot slipped, her legs flew out from under her, and she sat, splat, in the middle of a mud puddle.

"Jane!" He leaped from the buckboard. "Are you all right?"

She flapped her arms, rocking with laughter. "I'm fine. I'm a mud hen, don't you know."

He shook his head. "Too pretty for that. A bluebird, maybe." He stuffed Becca's letter into his pocket and scooped Jane up in his arms. "At least you're not hurt." Slogging across the muddy street, he deposited her on the front stoop of the sheriff's cottage.

Still giggling, she leaned against him as she stepped out of her muddy galoshes to expose dainty patent leather slippers with pointy toes.

Always in fashion!

Peter couldn't help smiling.

Cleaning his boots on the boot scraper by the door, he followed her into the charming little parlor. It was so typically Jane with its lace curtains, embroidered antimacassars on the rose-colored Victorian chairs and couch, and the porcelain figurines of birds and flowers artfully arranged among books and things that reflected a man's presence, as well.

Peter sniffed the warm, spice-filled air. "Smells good in here."

"I told you. I made your favorite ginger cookies." While she chattered, she slipped out of her soggy cape, holding it delicately away from her. "I guess everything else is clean." Her blond curls fell across her cheek as she twisted to examine the back of her gray pleated skirt. "I baked a mince pie, too, that I was going to take to Mrs. Meade. She's been under the weather lately and needs some cheering up. But I can make her another one. You'll take this one home for your and Uncle Jacob's supper. . . . Here, give me your jacket; I'll clean off the mud."

"While you're about it, you might look in the mirror." He brushed a smudge off her nose. "Never mind, that did it."

"Anything else that isn't perfect?" she said with mock primness, pirouetting for his inspection.

"No, I'd say you look just fine."

She curtsied coyly. "You go sit down in front of the fire and warm yourself. I won't be a minute!" she called back, disappearing into the kitchen.

He could hear the tap of her slippered feet on the wood plank floor of the back porch, water splashing into a tin bucket, and her soft lilting voice, singing, " 'I came to the garden alone while the dew was still on the roses,' " as she went about her task. It reminded him of Aunt Faith's hymn humming, and he smiled.

There was a different feel about a house with a woman living in it.

He relaxed into the overstuffed chair, which was obviously the sheriff's, and stretched out his legs onto the matching ottoman. There was a quiet serenity to this little cottage. It reflected Jane, but it accommodated a man's comfort.

He sighed. How easy it would be for some fellow to fall into the habit of loving Jane. She was so genuinely sweet, so home-centered, so domestic.

If Jane was a bluebird, small and soft, all chirp and flutter, feathering her nest, his Becca was a swan, splendid and full-breasted with a slender neck and regal bearing, floating on the narrow river of her destiny.

He smiled at the comparison.

"Your jacket looks as good as new," Jane chirped, dancing past him to hang it on a hook near the door.

"Thank you, Janie."

"It was the least I could do, seeing as it was my fault it got dirty."

"A taste of those good cookies is compensation enough." He heaved himself out of the chair and ambled after her to the kitchen. He leaned against the door frame, watching her as she stoked the fire under the simmering cider, reached on tiptoes for china-painted plates and cups, and placed the linen napkins on the silver tray that had belonged to Aunt Faith.

It gave him pleasure to see it being used and enjoyed again. Jane looked up from cutting a nut-filled fruitcake. "I haven't heard from Becca since Christmas, but I know I will soon." She arranged the slices next to the ginger cookies. "Fruitcake's better now than it was at Christmas, more aged," she remarked, dusting the slices with powdered sugar. "I'll bet Becca was thrilled with the microscope."

She opened a flat tin and extracted squares of dark fudge and pale fondant, filling a small cut-crystal dish.

He knew he should tell her not to go to so much trouble, but it was so friendly watching her flit around the kitchen, fussing just for him.

Comforting to know there was at least one person who didn't think of him as a brother.

"Yes, I'd say the microscope was a hit."

She poured cider into a silver pitcher.

Peter straightened. "Let me," he said, reaching for the tray.

"Why, thank you, kind sir." She smiled up at him. "Just put it on the small table between the chairs in the parlor."

He did as he was instructed then settled again into the sheriff's chair. Jane perched on the Victorian one opposite him. She passed him a napkin and a plate.

"This is pretty," he said, examining the plate.

"I'm glad you like it. I painted the set myself. Pastor David's wife taught a china-painting class at church last year." She poured cider into a matching cup and handed it to him.

He closed his eyes, inhaling the rich smell of cinnamon and nutmeg as he took a sip of the steaming brew. "Mmm."

"Mama's recipe. So are the cookies."

He took another swallow and sat back in the chair, savoring the taste as it slid down his throat. "Warms the cockles. Your papa was a lucky man to have a wife with such cooking skills."

"Papa tells me I inherited her talent."

"Well then, it'll be a lucky fella who gets you, too, Janie."

"I hope he'll think so," she said softly, her eyes lowered.

There was a moment of silence that verged on awkward until she said, "So, do you think Becca's sweet on that Winston fellow?"

Peter's fingers tightened around the handle of his cup.

"She mentions him a lot in her letters."

His stomach clenched.

"He was really there for her when she needed a friend. Helping her get into medical school and all."

"I think Becca is intelligent enough to have made it on her own," he murmured, struggling to contain his emotions.

"Of course she is," Jane replied brightly. "Still, it couldn't have hurt, his grandpa being the chairman of the board of trustees and all." She helped herself to a ginger cookie. "Winston Fullrider. I must admit, the name does have a certain ring: money, influence. From what she said, half the town, even the university, has the name *Fullrider* written on it somewhere."

"I get her letters, too," he snapped, momentarily losing the emotional battle.

Jane didn't seem to notice. She took a bite out of her cookie, chewed, and swallowed. "But she says he's very nice"—she smiled—"anyway."

"No doubt," Peter said glumly.

"Becca isn't one to be swept off her feet by superficialities"—Jane giggled—"such as prestige, influence, intelligence, money." She nibbled her ginger cookie. "And I gather he's quite handsome."

Peter frowned. "You sure know a lot about him."

"That's what girls write about to their girlfriends, not their papas and brothers."

I'm not her brother. I wish someone would acknowledge that!

"More cider?" Jane reached for his cup. "So, what else did Becca have to say in her letter, other than that she liked the microscope?"

"Not much. She had a paper due. In anatomy." *Winston was taking her to the library.* "She said she'd write more later."

"She's so smart and intellectual. When you think about it, it's quite amazing that we're best friends."

"What do you mean? You're plenty smart, Jane," Peter said, grateful to change the subject. "Besides, folks are smart in different ways. Becca's not nearly the cook you are, and as for tatting, you remember Aunt Faith tried to teach her and she's all thumbs. . .although she does knit pretty well," he added, feeling suddenly defensive of the woman he loved. Then he smiled. "And she doesn't shoot a gun nearly as good as you do. In fact, I think it's high time your daddy deputized you."

Jane tilted her head. "Why would he do a thing like that?"

"Rumor has it, you're a better shot than he is." Peter put down his cup. "Imagine, a little thing like you. Why, the gun's bigger than you are."

"I was blessed with a natural talent," Jane said modestly. "And of course it didn't hurt that Daddy wanted a boy, so I got to do all the fun things with him he would have done with a son."

"You're still all girl, Miss Jane. Whispering Bluff's own Annie Oakley. It's probably a good thing you are a good shot. A pretty little gal like you who can cook and sew and is so skilled in the womanly arts needs protection. What better protection than a Winchester rifle."

"Protection is one thing. Scaring a good man off is another."

Peter stood up. "Scaring 'em off is your daddy's job."

"I'd hate to think he'd scare you off, Peter."

Peter laughed. "Not as long as you keep baking those ginger cookies. Well, I'd better be on my way. Still have to pick up some things at Thompson's and stop by the feed store. Don't want to get on the road after dark."

He smiled down at her. "It's really been nice, Jane. Thank you for inviting me in."

"You know you're always welcome," she murmured, taking his jacket from the hook and holding it out to him.

"Give my regards to the sheriff," he said, taking it from her. "And be sure you tell him for me not to scare those beaux away."

"You know I'm not looking to collect a string of them, Peter. I'm not a trophy hunter."

"I know you're not, Jane."

"All I need is to find one good one."

"And lucky he will be, too."

Her large, lavender eyes held such vulnerability, such naked longing, it made him uneasy. . .and a little sad.

She lowered her gaze. "I'm real glad you dropped by, Peter. It doesn't seem as if you come as often as you used to."

He shrugged into his jacket. "I suppose that's so. Uncle Jacob and I have been making some plans for the farm. We're going to work more of the land ourselves, experiment with some new crops come spring."

"It isn't spring yet. . . . I miss seeing you now that Becca's gone. We used to have such fun, the three of us."

"We did."

"Maybe the two of us could—oh my!" Her hands flew to her cheeks. "The pie, I almost forgot."

He touched her arm. "Give it to Mrs. Meade. She needs it more than we do right now. I'll get ours next time."

"When is that, Peter? Next week?"

He gazed down into her sweet face. Not wanting to answer but knowing he must. He sighed inwardly, conquered by her innocent trust.

"Sure. Next week."

fifteen

One might have thought the frantic days would have been the most difficult for Becca, but it was the nights—wrapped in darkness, the midnight silence punctuated by the creaks and groans of the old house, footsteps in the hall, a door closing. Bone weary, she would lie staring into the blackness, her brain a kaleidoscope of facts, theorems, analyses, equations. These were the loneliest hours, when only thoughts of home calmed her mind and fed her soul.

Then there was the Lord!

Despite her issues with Him, she'd come to realize that she could not make the journey alone and often came back to Deuteronomy 31:6. "Be strong and of a good courage, fear not, nor be afraid. . .for the Lord thy God, he it is that doth go with thee; he will not fail thee, nor forsake thee."

As a result, she remained undaunted. When her fellow students flagged or faltered, she forged ahead; when they were discouraged, she persevered. Only to Papa and Peter did she ever complain, and then only in a light or humorous vein. What could they do so far away?

With God's help, adversity had made her strong, ridicule had made her impervious. Consequently, as she approached the completion of her first year, much to the chagrin of her male counterparts, Becca was unchallenged at the top of her class.

Grumble as they might, it was doubtful any of them had sacrificed the pleasures and friendships that she had to attain her goal.

Her rigorous schedule of lectures, lab assignments, research projects, case studies, patient rounds, and all the rest that was expected of a first-year medical student had left her little time for a social life. She enjoyed an occasional dinner with her friend Winston, a coffee break or brief lunch between classes, and evenings when they studied side by side in the silence of the library and drove home in his phaeton with the top down in the spring night, the stars pointing the way back to Mrs. Gotts's Boardinghouse (the good woman herself keeping a sharp eye on the curfew).

Winston made no bones about the fact that he had a special affinity for her and, Becca had to admit, she for him. What young lady wouldn't? With his good looks and genuine charm. . .and the wherewithal to bring a girl flowers when the occasion demanded—which was often enough. But even if she'd had the inclination, she didn't have the time to participate in the endless social obligations that filled his life and the pages of the *Boulder Gazette*.

As the last male Fullrider to carry the name, his destiny was defined from birth: first law and then politics. Governor Winston Fullrider. Senator Winston Fullrider. His future held no limits.

Hers lay in Whispering Bluff as Rebecca W. Hostettler, MD.

Two diverse roads that for a time converged.

And yet. . .and yet, in brief, pensive moments, those moments when she was most weary, most vulnerable, most lonesome for home, thoughts crept in of what a future with Winston Fullrider might be like. Thoughts that she quickly dismissed!

Her only other social interaction was over the dining table in Mrs. Gotts's Boardinghouse, with Mrs. Gotts presiding, Colonel Higby holding forth on matters of the utmost unimportance, humorous asides from her chum, Grace Preen, and Miss Tattler's sly commentary on the upper crust of Boulder society in which the Fullriders played a prominent role.

One Friday afternoon, near the end of the term, Becca managed to find time to join Mrs. Gotts, Miss Tattler, and

Grace in the parlor for Mrs. Gotts's ritual of refinement, afternoon tea.

Miss Tattler, seated in one of the upright Victorian chairs by the front window, raised red-rimmed black eyes above her pince-nez as Mrs. Gotts greeted Becca.

"So glad you could join us, dear." Mrs. Gotts poured tea into one of her delicate china cups from the teapot on her antique silver service, adding a spot of cream and a half teaspoon of sugar—by now she knew her guests' habits.

"Thank you, Mrs. Gotts." Becca took the proffered cup, helped herself to a sugar cookie, and sat down next to Grace on the sofa facing the fireplace.

Miss Tattler put down her cup with a clink, squirmed in her chair, and dabbed her lips several times with her napkin, glancing all the while at the folded newspaper on the table beside her. Good manners kept her from picking it up, but her twitching hands made it obvious she could hardly wait to share the contents.

Becca obliged. "So, what's new on the social scene, Miss Tattler?" *Though I don't care a whit.*

How apt the woman's name.

Grace gave a belabored sigh. "Must you?" she muttered under her breath.

Becca only grinned.

"Interesting you should ask." The mousy little woman gave Becca a sly, sidelong glance as she picked up the paper. " 'Stepping Out' has devoted most of the column to someone you know *quite* well."

"And who might that be?" *As if I can't guess.*

"It seems your swain, Mr. Winston Fullrider, is swimming with some other swan. Would you like me to read the column aloud?" Miss Tattler's little eyes gleamed with anticipation.

"Really, Miss Tattler," Grace erupted, in obvious concern for her friend's feelings. "Who cares about such nonsense?"

"Ladies, please," Mrs. Gotts interjected.

"No, no. I am interested, Miss Tattler," Becca said, curious about Winston's currently documented antics.

Becca was fully aware of his activities. Had she been the only girl Winston courted, indeed, he would have had a scant social life to be written about.

Still, she felt a twinge as Miss Tattler eagerly began. " 'All eyes at the Boulder Country Club Spring Cotillion turned as Miss Emily van Pelt entered the ballroom on the arm of the ubiquitous Winston Fullrider, scion to the Fullrider fortune. Miss van Pelt is the daughter of industrialist Charles Edward van Pelt and granddaughter of Senator Arnold Brimer, on her mother's side.

" 'Miss van Pelt's gown of pale blue–dotted crepon, trimmed with lace at the throat, a slight train with matching lace flounce at the hem, and a washed-silk sash of deeper blue, was in the highest fashion, a complement to her delicate blond beauty and luminous blue eyes.' "

Miss Tattler glanced up and then continued. " 'Miss van Pelt, an accomplished artist, fluent in three languages, is on vacation from her studies at the Sorbonne in Paris. When queried about her long-standing relationship with Mr. Fullrider, Miss van Pelt insisted, "We remain just friends," giving this columnist, for one, pause to wonder if the lady "doth protest too much." ' "

Miss Tattler squinted over her pince-nez, giving Becca a what-do-you-say-to-that? look.

No way was she going to give the little gossip the satisfaction of anything but the most benign response. "Emily is lovely. I met her through Winston," Becca responded airily, making it sound as if they were the best of friends. "I didn't realize she spoke three languages, though. That is impressive."

Miss Tattler cleared her throat and frowned. Obviously Becca's reaction was not at all what she had hoped for.

The ring of the doorbell spared her from further disappointment. . .and Becca from further improvisation.

Miss Tattler, who could see out to the front door from where she sat, murmured, "I declare, the devil himself."

"I hardly think so," Becca replied staunchly, jumping up

and striding to the front door. She threw it open with a flourish. "Winston! You're famous!" she cried, ushering him into the room and brushing his cheek with a quick kiss, a public display of affection that, as a rule, was quite against her nature. But under the circumstances. . . The expression on Miss Tattler's face made it worth it. "Miss Tattler has been regaling us with your publicity."

Dear Winston. He sized up the situation at once and turned to the little woman who was shrinking down into the plush of her Victorian chair. "Ah, Miss Tattler," he said, tilting his head and giving her the flirtatious Fullrider grin. "I do hope the photograph was flattering."

Grace giggled, her teacup clattering in its saucer.

Miss Tattler pursed her lips. "Indubitably!" She lifted her cup.

"How could it be otherwise?" Becca chortled, squeezing his hand.

"Tea, Mr. Fullrider?" Mrs. Gotts inquired.

"Thank you very much, but no thank you, Mrs. Gotts. I'm just here for a few minutes to see my Becca." He winked.

Becca drew him into the library alcove and pulled him down onto the window seat beside her, discreet but closer than she usually allowed, just in case Miss Tattler's curious gaze shifted in their direction, which she knew it would.

"What's going on?"

Becca shrugged. "You know Miss Tattler and her obsession about society. Especially yours."

"Who can blame her? I'm so very fascinating," he said archly.

"This time you were." Becca lifted a brow. "But I'm afraid she didn't get the response from me that she'd counted on."

"And what was that?"

"What do you think?"

"Jealousy, I hope."

"Do you think I'd admit it?"

"Probably not."

"Why would I be jealous anyway? You already told me you

were going to the cotillion. . .to please your mama. You just didn't mention that it was Emily van Pelt you were taking."

"Would it have made a difference?"

"Of course not. She being such an ugly duckling and all. Only a Good Samaritan like you would do her the favor. At the urging of your mama, of course. I'm sure the famous Fullrider smile in the photograph only hid your misery."

Winston sighed. "Becca, Becca, what am I going to do with you? It would be nice to think you cared enough to pine for me just a little."

Becca tossed her head. "I would, but I haven't the time."

Winston's expression sobered. "Would you laugh if I told you there were times when I pine for you?"

"What? Did Emily turn out to have two left feet? But then, you already knew that."

"I mean it, Becca."

She gave him a keen look, searching for the teasing twinkle in his eyes. . .but found it missing.

"I wouldn't laugh," she said quietly.

For a long moment, he continued his silent gaze then shook his head, as if clearing his clouded senses, and reverted to a winning smile. The charming rogue again. "I was sent to invite you to Sunday dinner."

"What? My goodness." She was too surprised to know how to react. "That's out of the blue."

"Grandfather says it's high time he had a look at you."

"Well. . .wh–why?"

"He's been following your progress."

"Oh my!" Becca swallowed. She took a deep breath. This was a strange turn of events. A frightening one!

"He says he wants to meet the lady whose academic perform-ance has saved his reputation. He did put in a good word for you, remember."

"Thanks to you."

"I just gave him a nudge."

"And what did you know about me?"

"Very little, I suppose. I guess I went on faith"—he grinned—"and beauty."

"Faith for sure. On your grandfather's part, as well."

"He believes in that kind of thing."

"Don't you?"

"In your case, yes."

"But not always."

He shrugged. "I don't think about it much—hey, don't look so scared. Grandfather's not an ogre." Winston grinned. "He only acts like one."

"That's heartening."

"Not to worry. I'll be there." He reached out and took her hand, continuing to grasp it as they walked back through the parlor.

"Good afternoon, ladies."

"Next time, you must join us for tea, Mr. Fullrider," Mrs. Gotts said.

Grace Preen smiled, and Miss Tattler nodded, a slightly self-conscious expression on her little pinched face.

At the front door, Winston, still holding Becca's hand, paused. "So, church starts at eleven. I'll pick you up at ten thirty. That ought to give us enough time to get there."

"Church? I didn't know you bothered to go to church."

"Certainly I go to church. I just don't make a big thing about it. I go at Easter and Christmas and"—he smiled down at her—"any other time my family pressures me into it."

"And this is one of those times?"

"No." He looked down at her, his expression serious again. "No, this is not one of those times. I have my own reasons."

He squeezed her hand, released it; then he turned and loped down the front steps.

sixteen

June 18, 1899

Dear Papa and Peter,

Sorry it's been so long since I've written, but there's been so much to wrap up this last month—two papers, three oral exams, which I feel went very well—and now only my written finals. I intend to stay #1 in the class. (Fusty old Dean Dodd still won't meet my eye when we pass in the hall. It gives me satisfaction.)

One person I don't have to prove anything to is Winston. He remains, as always, my stalwart champion and friend. Really more than a friend, which I didn't anticipate. That's one of the main reasons for this letter.

Two Sundays ago, I met his family: his mother and father, his two sisters, Anna and Eve, and his grandfather, Winston Edward Fullrider I, who—are you sitting down?—wanted to meet "the young woman who had put the men on their mettle." His words.

Winston picked me up for church. His, not mine. He was late, as usual, and so by the time we arrived, there were only a few stragglers like us hurrying up the marble steps. That's right, marble *steps*, lots of them, and two bell towers, and double carved doors two-stories high, leading into the narthex, where we were met by an army of ushers (almost as many as the number of members in Good Shepherd Church) wearing dove gray morning coats with tails, pinstripe trousers, and white flowers in their buttonholes.

We were led into a sanctuary grand enough to hold at least two of our little church in Whispering Bluff. If I'd been a turtle, I'd have popped my head back into my shell,

*but not Winston; he followed the usher down the mile-long
aisle, smiling and nodding to folks he recognized—like the
politician he one day hopes to be.*

*Finally, finally. we reached the Fullrider pew—I knew
it from the discreet bronze plaque bearing the family name,
FULLRIDER—in the very FIRST ROW!*

*I got the feeling even Moses would think twice about
trespassing.*

*Dr. Fullrider, very distinguished, was seated next to the
middle aisle, Winston's father beside him, and then his mother,
his two sisters, Anna and Eve, myself and Winston on the
end. The Fullriders are a stylish, handsome clan, which didn't
surprise me, judging from Winston's fine looks.*

*Before the service began, I had time to be awestruck by
the beauty of Grace Church (that Dr. Fullrider founded!).
Rainbows of light shimmered from stained glass windows,
a gilded cross floated in front of the richly carved reredos
behind the altar, and two intricately carved lecterns flanked
the chancel.*

But where was the organ? Where was the choir?

I was soon to find out.

*Suddenly great chords stilled the murmuring congregation,
and angelic voices soared like a silvery stream over the
sanctuary. I turned and looked up. Beneath a rose window,
cardinal-robed choirboys filled a loft that seemed suspended
between the grand organ's pipes.*

Do I wax poetic? How else can I explain it?

*Then the music segued into a hymn (unfamiliar), the
congregation rose—as Winston shuffled through the pages in
the hymnal—and before a lifted cross, the clergy, in elegantly
embroidered vestments, processed down the center aisle.*

*The liturgy was unfamiliar, too, but I noticed that Winston
was often as confused as I, a clue to the infrequency of his
attendance. As for the sermon, I'm sure it was heartfelt and
profound, but it was lost on me in all the pageantry.*

What a contrast to what I am used to. I must admit, grand

and glorious as it all was, I personally felt closer to our Lord beneath the tiny steeple of our own dear little Good Shepherd Community Church in Whispering Bluff.

I'm happy to say, however, that there was one familiar note. . .well, several. The service ended with "The Church's One Foundation," in which I joined lustily.

When we came out, folks were already gathered on the portico and down the marble steps, waiting for their carriages: gentlemen in frock coats and top hats, ladies in rustling silk and rose-trimmed bonnets, gossiping, preening, more intent, it seemed, on scrutinizing each others' outfits (or showing off their own) than on the substance of the sermon.

Still, everyone to whom Winston introduced me was so nice and greeted me with such welcoming kindness I quite forgot my modest navy dress and simple boater. Everyone, that is, except his sister Anna, who looked at me from head to toe with a gaze of mild condescension.

I was later to realize that was her usual expression.

The Fullrider mansion turned out to be almost as elaborate as the church, only somewhat smaller. The entry hall was so hushed and elegant, with its burnished oak floors, vaulted ceilings, Tiffany chandelier, and leaded glass windows, that I felt like whispering.

A maid, dressed more fashionably than I, ushered us into the parlor.

As I entered, Dr. Fullrider stepped forward and—would you believe?—KISSED MY HAND! I could have swooned. Winston's charm and good looks are definitely genetic. Dr. Fullrider is a tall, imposing gentleman with a shock of white hair and well-trimmed beard and penetrating dark eyes beneath beetle brows that make him look quite lionesque, but his smile is as winsome as Winston's.

Winston's parents, too, gave me a warm welcome, his mother regal and blond, his father a replica of Winston with the added bulk of years. His sisters, on the other hand, Anna, blond as her mother, and Eve, slender and dark, were—how shall I put it?—painfully polite.

And then, the maid announced dinner.

The dining room was equally dazzling with a blinding display of crystal, flowers, candelabras and sterling silver place settings lined up like small armies on either side of the silver chargers. And a use for every piece, with more courses than I could count. Thank goodness Mama taught me to wait for the hostess when in doubt about which implement to use. Otherwise I would have been lost.

Through dinner Mrs. Fullrider impressed me with an inventory of her activities. She is the current chairman of the Debutante Ball. She didn't really want the responsibility except that this is the year her daughters will be formally introduced to Boulder society, and she wanted it to be done right. She's also on the altar committee at church and president of the Orphanage Guild in which the members donate their used clothing—which conjured a picture of orphans in boas and top hats that made me giggle inside.

Winston's father is a member of the church vestry and active in Golfers for God, a weekly prayer breakfast held at his country club.

The conversation then turned toward me.

Winston's father asked what business you were in, Papa. When I told him you were a farmer, Winston's sister Eve offered that their grandfather on their mother's side owned a ranch. Anna added that it was three thousand acres and waited for my response.

I took a sip of soup.

With a not-so-subtle glare at his granddaughter, Dr. Fullrider jumped into the breach, asking me questions about school, how I was being treated, what I thought of my professors, to which I gave candid but, hopefully, tactful answers. At which point, he said he wished his granddaughters would do something useful with their lives instead of focusing on debutante balls and fashion statements *and snaring an eligible young man to sustain the lifestyle in which their parents have indulged them.*

Which seemed a rather harsh criticism of Mr. and Mrs. Fullrider's parenting, but they seemed to take his remarks in stride.

Dr. Fullrider continued, saying that they should be developing their talents, making something of themselves, "like Becca here."

I could have dropped under the table. You can imagine how that *endeared* me to the sisters. Anna cast me a cool glance and reminded her grandfather that she was taking watercolor lessons and Eve, piano.

Clearly, Dr. Fullrider does not think his family is meeting the mark. But I was surprised he would express himself with such candor in front of a guest.

And still he wasn't finished with them. He went on to suggest that his son, Winston's father, spent less time practicing law than his golf swing. When he was his son's age, Dr. Fullrider said, he was grubbing in the mines at Leadville.

Mr. Fullrider reminded him that actually he had already built a fortune and donated the money for Fullrider Hall.

Dr. Fullrider pointed out that even so, at ninety-three he still worked in his office five days a week.

I was impressed by that and asked where his office was located.

"Two floors down," Winston murmured dryly.

Winston's father said that some folks' hobby is their work, for other folks it's golf. As a young lawyer, he said, he'd paid his dues; now as a senior partner, his adjunct office was his club where he played golf, entertained, and cultivated clients. . .which, he pointed out, wouldn't hurt Winston's chances when he went into politics—apparently a foregone conclusion in the Fullrider family.

Dr. Fullrider responded that he was also concerned that his grandson seemed less focused on practicing law than jumping straight into the senior partner phase of golf and entertaining, *judging from what he'd recently been reading in the social columns.*

I felt as if I'd been watching a tennis match, back and forth, back and forth, but this ball was out of bounds! Someone had to stand up for Winston.

I told Dr. Fullrider I didn't think that was fair; after all, Winston was at the top of his class.

The old man looked bemused but, to my surprise, not affronted by my audacity, and he responded that he hadn't said Winston wasn't smart; it was his work ethic that was of concern.

Winston rolled his eyes and went on eating. Apparently they'd all heard this before.

Undaunted, the old gentleman continued about Winston needing a strong woman to anchor him, someone with character and drive. Anna broke in, agreeing with her grandfather for the first time. Yes, she said, someone of similar background (I didn't need to be all that smart to figure that one out), who knew how to entertain, was comfortable in society, could be a helpmate rather than promoting her own career (another flash).

Mrs. Fullrider suggested it was time for dessert.

I must say, when it was all over, I felt like a limp dishrag. On the way home, Winston apologized for his sisters' behavior, especially Anna's.

I assured him he needn't, that families were that way.

But not mine. Thank You, God!

And then he said his grandfather had taken him aside and told him I was a girl he shouldn't let get away.

Of course I laughed and said I doubted he'd get the same consensus from his sisters. But he said he valued his grandfather's opinion more. He said it lightly, but I could see he was serious.

And then he told me that his grandfather had only confirmed what had been in his own thoughts and heart for a long time. Now that Winston was graduating, starting his

*practice of law, beginning a new chapter in his life, he needed
to know where my heart lay.*

Well, Papa and Peter, I know where my heart lies. I love him.

*He sees in me what you do: not what I am but what I
can be, a woman of courage and strength, with focus and
conviction.*

*He brings out the best in me, as I think I do in him. We fill
in the gaps for each other. I ground him, he gives me courage;
I challenge him, he gives me confidence; I help him find focus,
he gives me whimsy. And he appreciates me as a woman.
What a gift that is.*

*Oh, I know, there are differences—if anything this letter
illuminates them—his family, his faith, even his ambitions.
But what relationship doesn't have its challenges? And doesn't
surmounting them bring strength? We love each other, and
that's what's most important.*

*And don't worry, Papa, if I were to marry Winston, I
would still become a doctor. He understands that. Like you,
he's always encouraged my achievement. That's one of the
things I appreciate and love about him. And I'd still practice
where I'm needed most, albeit not in Whispering Bluff but
some poor area here.*

*We've decided to wait until I return from vacation before
any betrothal announcement. Actually, I've decided, and he's
reluctantly agreed. Dear soul, he says he's afraid to take the
risk of losing me. (Small chance, given the limited choices
in W.B., although I didn't tell him that.) Winston is more
impulsive than I. I need time to sort things out.*

*Well, that's it in a nutshell. Are you too shocked? In
thinking back, I suspect I've given you plenty of clues. It was
I who was clueless.*

*I'm counting the days when I'll see you. Until then, pray for
me as I pray for you.*

Love,
Becca

seventeen

" 'Pray for me as I pray for you. Love, Becca.'" Peter tried to keep the emotion out of his voice as he finished reading Becca's letter to Jacob. But it was hard when his heart had just been ripped to shreds. His dreams demolished!

It was late Friday afternoon, the week before she was to arrive home. Jacob was lounging on the porch swing, whittling, ice melting in the half-empty glass of lemonade on the table beside him. Peter squatted on the front steps, his gaze locked on the pages in his hand, his stomach coiled with tension.

"I love him," she'd said. *"I love him. I love him."*

It hurt even to breathe.

"I love him."

In the lengthening shadows, bees droned lazily in the twining roses, and through the kitchen window floated the sounds of Helga's busyness as she cleaned up before heading home. Behind him, the springs of the porch swing squealed in discordant monotony as Jacob rocked back and forth, back and forth, until Peter thought he'd jump out of his skin. How could everything sound so normal when there was such chaos in his heart?

For several minutes, neither he nor Jacob spoke.

Jacob leaned forward. "What are you thinking, Peter?"

Peter's reaction was sharp. Unwarranted. He couldn't help it. He didn't want to help it. That was the crux of it. He wanted to suffer. He had a right to suffer. Lick his wounds. Be left alone. "What do you think I'm thinking?"

"You tell me," Jacob said, rising.

Peter crumpled the letter and stood up.

Jacob waited.

"I'm thinking it's too late," he muttered. "I'm thinking I've missed my chance. If I ever had one."

"I was afraid you'd say that."

"Then why ask?"

Jacob looked down at him from the step above. "Because I sensed you didn't hear the same thing I heard, Peter."

"How could it have been clearer? She's in love with that Winston fellow."

"What I heard was a girl trying to convince herself."

"It didn't sound that way to me. It sounded like a girl who intends to get married."

"Then why the litany of reasons she shouldn't?" With an unusual abruptness, Jacob leaned down and grabbed the letter. He smoothed it on his thigh and flipped through the pages until he found the passage he sought, pointed to the paragraph, and read, " 'Oh, I know, there are differences—if anything this letter illuminates them—his family, his faith, even his ambitions.' " He snorted. "What kind of foundation is that for a marriage?"

"Obviously she's willing to take the risk. It seems love conquers all," Peter said bitterly.

"That's a girl talking, not a woman." Jacob thrust the letter back into Peter's hand and folded his arms. "She may be smart, but she's still a girl." He looked out toward the orchard. "The isolation, the ridicule, no family near to give her support, to give her balance. No wonder she grabbed the first lifeboat in the storm."

"More like a yacht," Peter muttered.

Jacob turned, his face a tempest of emotions. "If you'd had the gumption to stand up and tell her how you felt in the first place, this might never have happened."

Peter was stunned. He had never seen the man so vociferous— or quite so impassioned.

Jacob continued. "Becca may be blind, but I'm not. I watch you pine and mope around here every time a letter from her arrives."

He'd always sensed Jacob was aware he had feelings for Becca, but the depth of them he'd tried to hide—apparently unsuccessfully.

"She's a determined, ambitious, self-centered girl," Jacob said, "who sees where she's heading, not where she is. All her life we've let her get away with it, given in to her, taken care of her—you especially, Peter. Now we're reaping the reward."

"Some reward."

"I care about you, Peter, but this is about my daughter. What do you think her life will be like if she marries into that family?"

"It doesn't matter what I think. It's her life," Peter said miserably, "and her choice."

"Well then give her more than one choice, son. It's about time you got some backbone." Jacob's tone was somewhere between anger and impatience. "She's coming home. There's still time. Tell her how you feel, boy. What do you have to lose?"

"Only my pride," Peter muttered, half to himself.

"Pride? Pshaw." Jacob gave him an assessing look. "You're not afraid, certainly?"

"Sure I'm afraid. I've been afraid all along. Why do you think I've put up with being her 'brother' all these years? I've been afraid I'd lose her completely, that I wouldn't even have what I have now."

"If she decides to marry this Winston boy, you won't have her anyway." He put his arm around Peter's shoulders. "Don't tell me that stuttering little sad-faced urchin who showed up at our door all those years ago had more courage than the man I'm seeing in front of me? I won't believe it.

"Look at you, lad. You're handsome, you're smart, you know that girl inside and out, better than she knows herself, and you understand how to handle her—which isn't an easy task, as we both well know. And you love her."

"More than my life."

"And she loves you—"

"Like a brother."

"Because that's the way you've treated her. You haven't given her a chance to know you any other way. Now you've got a month of chances. She'll be back home where she belongs. Her mind won't be clouded by distractions or values different from her own.

"Take the bull by the horns, Peter, before it really is too late. 'For God hath not given us the spirit of fear; but of power, and of love, and of a sound mind.' Make use of them!"

❧

A week later, Peter and Jacob stood on the station platform as the train from Denver wheezed to a stop, spitting steam beneath the chassis and giving a final blast from the whistle. The coach doors clanged open.

Barely had the porter set the step when Becca's foot was on it. In a spin of her blue skirt, her bowler at a tilt, almost before Peter could blink, she had thrown her arms around his neck, knocking his Stetson askew, and was slathering his face with kisses.

"Peter, Peter, Peter! I'm so glad to see you." Breathless, she stood back and surveyed him at arm's length. "I do declare! You are even more handsome than I remember. Why, look at you! I think you're taller, and your shoulders are broader for sure. And those muscles"—she squeezed his bicep—"my, my, now that I've passed anatomy, I can appreciate what a fine specimen of manhood you really are. If you weren't my brother, I'd go after you myself."

Peter caught Jacob's eye over her shoulder as she gave him another quick hug.

"Am I right, Papa? Isn't he gorgeous?" she exclaimed, turning. "And you! Look at you! Handsome as ever." Then she frowned, lifting a gloved hand to his temple. "Is that a gray hair? Surely I haven't given you cause for a gray hair? Or did Peter misbehave while I was gone?"

As she hugged her father, she stuck out her tongue at Peter then stepped back, clasping her hands in front of her. "Or do you both just look so beautiful to me because I love you so much and have missed you so much, and I am so glad to be home I can't even begin to tell you?" Finally, she ran out of breath.

"Well, my darling daughter," Jacob said, when he could get a word in, "we're plenty glad to see you, too, aren't we, Peter?"

"I think so!"

"You're not sure?" Becca grinned at him.

He smiled back. Time would tell. "I'll get your luggage."

He needed a respite from the sight of her flushed cheeks and her sparkling gray eyes with their glint of silver, from the touch of her lips and the scent of her. . . .

He needed to catch his breath.

He strode over to the baggage cart and yanked off her valise with the fervor of his frustration.

While Jacob fetched the carriage, Becca waited for Peter. Distracted by her own chatter, she stumbled on the bottom step of the platform's rickety stairs and would have fallen had he not been there to catch her.

She clung to him, laughing, and pasted a quick kiss on his cheek. "Always Peter, my rock. I'd hate to sprain an ankle. . . even though there is a doctor in the house. Or will be!"

It was all he could do not to throw down the valise, take her in his arms, and give her the welcome he'd dreamed about. And for an instant, just an instant, he very nearly did.

But Becca pulled free and Jacob arrived with the carriage, and the moment was past.

"Papa, you brought the phaeton."

"Of course I did, young lady. This is a special occasion."

Peter tossed the luggage in the backseat and helped Becca up beside her father.

"You're driving, son," Jacob said.

"I don't mind sitting in back," Peter said. In fact, he preferred it. Proximity to Becca was becoming increasingly unnerving.

"Nope." Jacob had already pushed the valise aside and slid into the backseat.

"You're sure?"

"You're driving," Jacob said firmly.

"Uncle Jacob—"

Becca gave a dry laugh. "Don't fight over me, gentlemen."

Shifting between reluctance and anticipation, Peter climbed into the front seat beside her.

For the hour it took to get back to the farm, Becca chattered endlessly, one arm over the back of the seat so she could talk to both her father and Peter at once. From time to time, she interrupted her breathless soliloquy as she recognized familiar landmarks: the mill, the schoolhouse, the church steeple in the distance.

"I can't wait to see Jane tomorrow," Becca said.

"She's invited us for dinner after church," her father said.

"I'll call her anyway when I get home." Becca giggled. "That way the whole community will know that Rebecca Hostettler has reached home safe and sound."

"The Pryce sisters' network," Jacob said.

"More like the Prying sisters' network." Becca laughed. "Speaking of Jane"—she gave Peter a sly smile—"how is she?"

"Fine, I guess. I haven't seen her in a while."

"I thought by now—"

He gave her a silencing glare.

"Oops. Have I hit a sensitive spot with the shy swain?" She tickled him under the chin.

He tried to swat her hand away, but like a persistent gnat, she continued until he grabbed her wrist and held it. "Cut it out." And held it, warm and pulsing in his hand, then thrust it away, turning his attention to the road.

She gave him a perplexed look, not quite hurt, and shrugged.

"Anyway," she continued, pointedly directing her comments to her father in the backseat, "Boulder is beautiful, but in a completely different way than here. How can I explain it? It's more ferocious: craggy rocks, rushing rivers, and the bustle of the busy city with its restaurants and lighted streets. I must say, it's exciting and stimulating. But there were so many times when I longed desperately for the wide-open spaces, the serenity of home. A place to feed my spirit and refresh my soul."

She shrugged. "But I suppose if I marry Winston—*when* I marry Winston—I'll get used to it. That won't be for a while, of course, with his establishing himself in his father's law firm and me in medical school. You'll like him, Papa. You, too, Peter." And she went droning on with a list of the man's virtues.

Peter tried not to hear, but her words infringed on him more and more, twisting the knife in his wounded heart, sending him deeper and deeper into despair as he realized the chance he'd hoped for, as Uncle Jacob put it, "to set her straight," was lost before she arrived.

ə

Becca settled in as if she'd never been gone, insisting on helping him and their new ranch hand, Gary, with the chores, accompanying Peter into town, promoting lunches with Jane.

"She's sweeter on you than ever, Peter," Becca said on their way home one afternoon. "I saw it Sunday at dinner, and today, how she looked at you. Oh, I know she's glad to see me but even gladder when you tag along. It's touching, really." Becca looked down at her hands and then back up at Peter. "You're certainly kind enough to her. But I'd hardly call you attentive. Honestly, Peter, I just can't understand why you're still so hesitant."

That did it!

Peter pulled the buckboard to the side of the road and reined in Henry. He turned and looked her in the eye. "I've had enough of your matchmaking!"

Becca returned an unwavering gaze. "You may not realize it now, Peter, but it's clear to me that Jane is perfect for you. I'm thinking of your happiness, and hers, too."

"I'm quite capable of determining my own happiness, Becca, as I'm sure you're capable of determining your own. So from now on, I expect you to mind your own business. Understood?"

He hardened his heart to the tears welling in her silver eyes. . .to the auburn curls brushing her pale brow. . .to the. . .

Abruptly he turned and snapped the reins.

"You're not being a bit nice," Becca said as old Henry lurched into a trot.

"So be it."

Becca turned away. He could feel the tension and hurt radiating from her. For rest of the journey home, she sat stiff and upright beside him, pondering her clasped hands.

In silence.

A blessing as he saw it!

The sun was just sliding behind the bluff when they pulled up to the barn. Above them, stars were gradually appearing in the twilit sky.

Gary hurried toward them and grabbed Henry's bridle as Peter hopped down and circled the buckboard to assist Becca.

"I don't need your help," she sniffed, brushing aside his proffered hand.

"Don't need it, or don't want it?" Peter muttered as he kept her from tumbling to her knees when her skirt caught on the heel of her boot.

She jerked her arm from his grasp, and with her back stiff as a cable, her head high, she strode toward the house.

Peter gazed after her.

He'd been wrong! Dead wrong to turn on her that way, venting his frustration. She didn't deserve it. In her mind, she'd been doing what she'd always done, watching out for him. . .being his loving. . .his loving. . .*sister*.

"Becca!" he called.

She didn't pause.

"Becca." He jogged after her. "Becca, I'm sorry. I shouldn't have talked to you that way. I had no cause." He caught up with her and touched her shoulder. "I know you have my best interests at heart."

She stopped and then turned. He could see she was crying.

She lowered her head and spoke in a tone so soft he had

to bend close to hear her. "Ever since I've been back, it's been different between you and me; things have changed. But I didn't want to admit it." She looked up at him beneath a tangle of wet lashes. "And now this. Oh, Peter, can't we just go back to how it was? Like I remember. . .like we used to be?" She put her hands up to her face. "I couldn't wait to come home," she murmured through muffled sobs, "and now. . .and now I'm so miserable."

What could he do but reach out and pull her into his arms, where she laid her head against his sadly thumping heart. What could he do but stroke her auburn curls, gleaming in the final rays of the sun? How could he help himself from feeling the soft, silky texture of her hair, the warmth of her lithe young body wrapped in his arms—from breathing in the sweet scent of her perfume?

How could he help from treasuring this moment of closeness, savoring it, storing it up to remember and bring out when she was no longer here?

"Please, can't it be the same?" she murmured against his cheek.

He couldn't answer her. The words wouldn't come. How could he tell her that it would never be the same again?

How could he tell her that if she married Winston, this moment was the best it would ever be?

eighteen

Things never did get back to the way they used to be between her and Peter. They shared some light moments, to be sure, but always there seemed a shadow between them.

Maybe she was overreacting. Maybe it was the pressure of his new responsibilities.

More and more, Papa had handed him the reins. And Peter had run with the challenge. He had hired new ranch hands, expanded their planting to the Jensen property they had purchased, and taken back the land cultivated by their tenant farmers. He was experimenting with new methods of plant rotation, new strains of alfalfa and sugar beets.

Yes, that had to be it. Even though he seemed to be taking it all in stride, it had to be a bit overwhelming. And he was working so hard.

Every evening he spent poring over journals, making notes on procedures, the newest organic fertilizers, innovative techniques. And certainly he was never rude. If she looked over his shoulder or made a comment or asked a question, he would always pause politely. But inevitably his reply was brief, and she sensed her presence was an interruption.

But even as she understood, or tried to, she was lonely, plain and simple. Lonely for the closeness and sharing between them that had been so unique and precious to her.

She wondered if he ever thought about those times as she did. And missed them.

So, she spent more hours with Papa, whose bout of arthritis had kept him chained to the porch swing. She put aside her chemistry and anatomy studies and instead read books from his library that he recommended. She puttered with Helga in the kitchen, took long walks in the orchard, climbed to the top of the grassy bluff where she sat under the stunted elm—alone—looked out over the plowed fields, and watched the little brook tumble over the rocks into the Rikums' pond next door.

She went to church on Sundays with Papa and Peter and to the Thursday night potlucks, and, of course, she spent some time with Jane. But life had gone on for Jane, too. She had her commitments as chairman of the Prayer Shawl Project, knitting warm shawls for the poor, as cochairman of the Christmas Bazaar, and on the Public Works Committee to pave Main Street.

The rhythm and flow of the Good Shepherd Church and the community of Whispering Bluff had continued without her.

It made Winston's letters especially precious when they arrived.

They were full of humorous descriptions of his antics with his university "brothers," his golf games, tennis trophies, rafting down the Colorado River, parties.

Boulder society was the opposite of that in Whispering Bluff, and if she didn't miss it, she at least missed him.

She felt adrift between two worlds, neither of which she seemed to fit into. And although her body and mind were refreshed from this respite from her studies, often her spirit lagged and her heart felt heavy.

She rode horseback for hours, drifting out through the tall grasses and sagebrush, past the windmills and along the westerly windbreak, then a half-mile farther along the river. She rode the familiar paths that she and Peter had ridden. Now she rode alone.

The solitude gave her time to think.

One afternoon, she tied Pegasus to the hitching rail beside the Good Shepherd Church and climbed the hill to the tiny graveyard and a view that spanned the whole valley.

From where she stood beside her mother's gravestone she could look down onto Main Street, make out the sign of

Thompson's General Store and the jail behind Jane's little cottage. She could see the post office and the bank and, on the other side of the street, Mavis Todd's Couture and Chapeaus, highfalutin names for "dressmaker and milliner." Becca smiled. Services her mama had never needed, unlike Becca who drew blood nearly every time she picked up a sewing needle.

To her left, she looked out toward the green-fringed Platte River and the beauty and fruitfulness that lay between it and the road leading home. In the distance, she could barely make out the top of the silo and, beyond their land, the Apples' family farm.

As far as she could see, golden wheat waltzed in the shimmering sunlight until it met the blue horizon. She almost felt as if her gaze followed the path Mama had taken into infinity.

As she stood there, a soft breeze, replete with the scent of zinnias and petunias, caressed her, and she wondered how anyone could deny a God who had created a universe of such impossible beauty...with the promise of even more to come.

She remembered the evening in front of the fire when Papa had so patiently explained that life here on earth was a jot in time compared to the hereafter. How her wrenching loss at Mama's passing was to God a mere stumble over the threshold from the finite of this world to the infinite of the next, with a beauty and peace beyond man's earthly comprehension.

With what God had already provided in this amazing universe, how could she doubt His plan for her future?

If she would let Him lead her!

For the first time since her mother had died, she accepted that God really did love her and knew what He was doing.

She began to appreciate God's gift of free will that brought with it difficult choices. Ultimately those choices had strengthened her faith and her resolve.

In that moment of meditative quiet beside her mother's grave, the familiar landscape over which she gazed gradually took on a grandeur and brilliance as she began to sense that her own small epiphany came wrapped in a certain peace.

❧

She, her father, and Peter had just finished a late supper and were polishing off the last of Helga's famous black bottom pie, when Becca reminded them, "I leave in just three days." She resisted the impulse to lick her fork. "It's hard to believe I've been here almost a month."

"I know." Her father gave her a fond smile. "I hate to think of your going."

"I hope you'll miss me, too, Peter," she said, with an oblique smile and arched brow.

He glanced up. "Of course."

"You've been so busy that I feel as if I've hardly seen you," she said.

"I'm sorry. Harvest time of year. You remember."

"I remember."

And I remember that you used to let me ride along beside you in the wagon.

"You'll have more time at Christmas," she said.

"I'm sure I will." He returned a quick, noncommittal smile and wiped his mouth with his napkin.

Becca rose and carried her plate to the sink. "Winston wrote that his parents gave him a trip to Europe as a surprise graduation present. He's leaving this week for two months." She sighed. "Which means, obviously, that he won't be there when I get back." She reached for her father's plate. "An exploration voyage before our own trip, he said. I suppose that was meant to console me." She laughed.

"And are you consoled?" Peter asked dryly.

"You must admit, it's kind of exciting to contemplate a European honeymoon."

"Yeah," Peter said, "like dangling a carrot."

Becca frowned at him. "He doesn't need to do that. . . . Anyway, I'm going to miss him."

"Lucky him." Peter pushed back from the table and stood up. "I've got chores to finish."

As the back door slammed, Becca murmured, "After sundown?"

She put her hands, palms down, on the drain board and looked out into the darkening yard.

He didn't head toward the barn.

Up until this moment she'd felt sad and disappointed; now anger began to simmer inside her. She swung around and faced her father. "That does it! This whole vacation he's been avoiding me. And now this! He was downright rude. He's no more going to do chores than I'm going to sing Carmen in the opera. You tell me what I said to get that kind of reaction?"

"You're absolutely right. That's not like him at all."

Becca crossed her arms. "And with no provocation! One would at least think he could be decent for another three days." She dropped down in the chair across from her father. "I don't understand it. We used to be so close. We did everything together; we finished each other's sentences. The joy for one of us was the joy for the other. Now, he's not interested at all in what I'm doing. If I so much as mention Boulder or school or Winston, he changes the subject so quickly it makes my head spin."

"Does he now? I wonder why that is."

"You tell me."

"Why don't you let him speak for himself? You're not one to let things go by, Becca," her father said. "If you think he's been acting like that since you arrived, I'm surprised you didn't satisfy your curiosity sooner."

"It's not curiosity, Papa. I'm hurt." Becca looked down at her hands. "I should have asked him before. I know it. But at first I thought maybe it was just me, being too sensitive. I made excuses for him. Now, it's been going on so long I'm afraid that if I do say something, he'll deny it and it'll just make matters worse." She picked at a loose thread on her skirt. "If I didn't know better, I'd say he was jealous of Winston."

Her father lifted a brow. "You think so?"

"It just occurred to me." She looked up. "When I think about it—no, Peter's not that way. I wish I wasn't such a sissy. I'd march right out there and make him tell me what his problem is!"

Her father intoned, " 'For God hath not given us the spirit of fear; but of power, and of love, and of a sound mind.' "

"I hear Mama speaking."

He smiled.

"You think I should do it?"

"Absolutely! I think you should clear the air between you two. He needs to know how you feel."

"Goodness, Papa, such vehemence isn't like you. Usually you don't get that involved in other folks' issues."

"Usually I think it's none of my business. But when it affects the two people I love most, maybe it is."

Becca looked toward the window. "I suppose I haven't much to lose. . .except that he may never speak to me again."

"Do you really think that?"

"No."

◆

She didn't bother to look in the barn. She knew that was the last place he'd be. She turned instead toward the bluff.

He stood on the crest above her, legs apart, arms akimbo, a lonely silhouette against the star-studded sky. He looked like some sad warrior, garbed in the silver armor of the moon, surveying his conquered land.

She wanted to be angry with him, but seeing him this way, it was hard. She sighed, struggling to rekindle the flame of her justified indignation.

Silently, stealthily, she climbed the hill, until she stood behind him.

"Peter!"

Startled, he swung around. "What are you doing here?"

"I might ask you the same, considering you said you were going to finish up your chores. Chores, Peter?"

"It was a polite way of saying I wanted to be alone."

"Well, too bad. Here I am."

"So I see." He looked less than happy.

"Unwelcome as I obviously am, I'm not going anywhere until I get some answers." She took his hand. "And neither are you!"

"There's no need to get physical, Becca."

She thrust his hand away.

"Where's your sense of humor?" he said dryly.

"I lost it when you stalked out of the kitchen tonight." She crossed her arms. "I suppose I shouldn't have been all that surprised. Since I've come home, you've spent as little time with me as you could get away with."

"Sorry if it seemed that way."

"Oh, please, Peter. It's me you're talking to. Remember? The person you vowed never to lie to."

He started to turn away. "Go on back to the house, Becca."

"No!" she said stubbornly.

"I really don't have anything to say."

"Then I'll talk," she said, stepping in front of him and barring his way.

He sighed. "Suit yourself."

She could almost hear the fingers of impatience tapping in his head.

So be it!

"I was gone almost a year, Peter. Or maybe you didn't notice."

"I noticed."

"That's a step in the right direction. Even if you didn't miss me."

"I didn't say that."

"Actions speak louder than words." She looked down at the grass. "Well, for your information. . .I missed you. I missed you a lot. I could hardly wait to get home and see you. I'd hoped—expected—you'd feel the same way."

She waited, giving him a chance to reassure her. Praying that he would.

When he didn't, she continued. "I thought things would get back to normal after we'd settled our little squabble about my matchmaking attempt. Obviously, they didn't." She shook her head. "Oh, Peter, I've needed you so much. I've needed you to talk to. . .to be playful with, like we used to be—"

"Playful!" He gave a derisive laugh. "We're not children anymore, Becca. We haven't got playtime."

"Stop it! Stop twisting my words with your sarcasm. You know what I mean: lighthearted, free, open with each other, honest—like we used to be. Not avoiding each other."

She felt close to tears and swallowed, struggling to contain her mounting emotion. "When I'm about to make the most important decision of my life, when I most need the warmth and understanding, the advice of the person I'm closest to in this whole world—or thought I was. . ."

She gave a small shuddering sigh. "You're my best friend, Peter, my soul mate, my. . .br—"

"Don't say it!"

The words exploded with force enough to make her take a step backward.

"I'm not your brother! I never have been! I never want to be! That's your fantasy, not mine. Which you might have figured out if everything wasn't always about *your* needs, *your* wants, *your* joy."

"Is that what you think?" She felt as if he had struck her.

"Why are you so upset, Becca? Your needs will still be met. Just by someone else." His voice held an obsequious insincerity. "It's not as if you're going to be alone. You'll have Winston. He's your confidant now. I'm not your soul mate anymore. That's what husbands are for."

What she'd said to Papa so offhandedly, what she didn't want to believe, he'd confirmed.

She was so sure he understood that there was no one she held dearer, that he had no competition for her affection. She'd always made a big point out of making that clear.

Why had she felt she had to?

"I think I've said all I need to," he said, beginning to move down the slope.

"You're jealous," she said with sad bemusement.

"Why would I be jealous?" he scoffed, his tone too strident.

"I'm so sorry. I didn't know."

"It seems you're the only one," he muttered.

It went deeper than jealousy. She could hear it in his voice, the raw, visceral sound of a man pulling words from deep inside himself. A man unwilling to take that next step, risk the humiliation of rejection by revealing the secrets of his heart.

She ached for him, for the pain she must have caused him.

He stood staring down at her, his fists clenched at his side, her hero, her silver warrior, if he only knew. But sadly, not in the way he wanted.

He sighed, let out his breath in one long, painful gasp, as if his whole body was deflating, losing its force. "Go back to the house, Becca." He turned and started down the back side of the bluff.

"Please talk to me."

He paused.

His words came over his shoulder, slow and soft, a sigh on the breeze. "What's the point? You made your choice. You've gotten on with your life. Congratulations! Now let me get on with mine."

"Don't turn your back on me!"

He continued down the hill.

"Don't do this."

He kept on walking.

"Don't walk away."

But he kept on, until he had disappeared into the dark, lacy labyrinth of the orchard.

"Don't walk away, you coward," she whispered.

nineteen

It had been a grim three days, she and Peter passing like strangers and poor Papa, the victim of their silent tension. The next two days on the train had been no better, battling her conflicting emotions as she sat staring out at the vast landscape.

She'd returned home with such high spirits and left in such misery.

Peter had ruined everything.

She had always trusted him. Now to find out that all these years had been a charade.

How could she get past the memories of shared confidences and dreams, the long walks on the bluff in the moonlight, sitting on the front steps staring at the stars?

All of it tangled up with Peter.

Tangled is right.

And all that time he'd loved her.

He'd shared everything but what was most important, what affected both their lives the most. *That* he'd kept secret.

How dare he!

How could he have been such a coward?

How could she have been so blind?

Or did she choose not to see?

Weary and disconsolate, she mounted the steps of Mrs. Gotts's Boardinghouse, dragging her valise and the even heavier burden of guilt and sadness. In her room, she dropped her cloche and coat into a careless heap on top of her valise and threw herself onto the bed.

Memories flooded over her like water over a breaking dam. She remembered that day in the buckboard, coming back from town when she'd chided him about Jane, the look he'd given her then—she remembered it, remembered that she'd noticed and dismissed it. She remembered the expression in his eyes when he'd call her *dulcet girl*, his silly, sweet name for her, and the tender way he'd treated her when Mama died.

So many memories.

And all the time he'd loved her, not like a brother but like a boy and then a man.

She'd taken him so for granted, like she took breathing and the beat of her heart.

How painful it must have been for him to keep that secret as he was sharing so many others.

If only he'd just been honest with her, told her the truth. Not felt he had to pretend.

But how would she have reacted? Would their friendship have risen to the heights that it had?

Or would she have, as he feared, ridiculed him and rejected him with the cruelty and carelessness of youth?

As the semester began, she threw herself into her studies, hoping to forestall her agonizing ruminations. But inevitably night came and with it, the plaguing guilt and doubts would begin all over again.

She realized, to her chagrin, that while she had been obsessing about Peter, she had entertained few thoughts of Winston. Wasn't he, after all, the most important person in her future?

Guiltily she began to concentrate on him instead, what their life would be like together: the grand house, the beautiful people, the prestigious church and country club, travel, the best private schools for their children—certainly not a little one-room schoolhouse with a flag pole and dirt play yard and a hitching post. . . . They would have the best. They would go to cotillions and take piano and art lessons. There would be banquets and parties and all the exciting activities in the life of a young politician and his family.

But where did "doctor" fit into this life?

There would be time for that, Winston had assured her,

with a nanny to care for their two children—a boy and a girl, according to his plan—and a cook and at least two maids: one for the upstairs and one for the down.

What more could a girl ask for?

Then why did she still toss and turn at night, suffering the agony of doubt?

Suddenly it came to her.

"Let God figure it out," Mama used to say.

Why didn't you speak up sooner, Mama?

In all her anxiety, she had forgotten the source of all understanding. What a dunce she had been to waste all this time.

In that moment of realization—more like remembering—she found herself able to release her guilt and uncertainty and open her mind to the presence of the Lord.

What a relief!

For the first time in many months, she drifted into a tranquil sleep and awoke the next morning with an inner peace that He had already provided her with clarity and understanding.

The answer had been there all along.

She saw Peter, clear as if he were standing before her, a man who would put his love of family above his own welfare and ambitions, a man who would nurture and love his children and not leave them in the care of others, a man who loved his neighbor as himself, and, above all, a man who loved God and was steadfast in His ways.

Peter, her soul mate!

What more could a girl ask for?

But even as her heart was filled with certainty and joy, it was clouded with sadness.

How was she going to break the news to Winston?

Once more, she would call on the Almighty. Between them, they had almost two months to work it out.

❧

"Young Mr. Fullrider's impending return was mentioned in the 'Stepping Out' column," announced Miss Tattler at the dinner table. To Becca's surprise!

The following day, she received a letter from Winston.

A week later, on the front page of the social section, his arrival at the Boulder train station was recorded in a three-column picture of a smiling Winston flanked by a coterie of family and friends.

Becca was not among them. No one had bothered to include her.

He dutifully called the night of his arrival and arranged to walk her home after class the following afternoon.

She was waiting in front of the lecture hall when he hurried up, breathless and apologetic.

"The brothers were celebrating my return. You know how it is. They were reluctant to let me leave." He gave her that special Fullrider grin.

She had to admit her heart did flutter.

If anything, he was more handsome than ever: his eyes bluer, his smile more engaging, and he seemed even taller, although she knew it wasn't so.

"You're looking lovely as always." He leaned over and gave her a swift kiss on the cheek.

Being a Fullrider, he was allowed a discreet public display of affection.

"Let me carry your books," he said, taking them from her.

Across the quad and down Elm Street, he continued an animated chronicle of his European escapades and included some of the sights he had seen, as well: the Colosseum in Rome, the Parthenon in Athens, the Palace of Versailles.

Becca offered an occasional "Hmm" or "Really?" or "My word, you didn't?"

He hardly paused or seemed to notice, much to her guilty relief. She was giving him only minimum attention as her mind was engaged with how. . .when. . .to tell him of her decision not to marry him, in the most graceful and least hurtful way.

"And how was Paris?" she asked absently. It wasn't until a number of steps farther that she realized he had stopped and was some paces behind. She turned.

He was standing quite still, looking somewhat embarrassed.

"Winston, what is it?"

"Oh, Becca, something has happened. . . . I didn't know how to tell you. I wanted to write, but. . ." His expression became more and more miserable. "In Paris. Remember my friend, Emily? Emily van Pelt? You met her. . ."

"Yes."

"Well, naturally, since we were old friends, I had to look her up—"

"Naturally."

"Of course, being old friends, she wanted to show me the sights, and we spent quite a bit of time together, and. . ."

Becca frowned. "What are you trying to say, Winston?"

"Well. That old spark between us was rekindled, burst into flame, you might say, and. . ." He took a deep breath. "And we're engaged. Formally! It's what our families always wanted. . . . Oh, Becca, I'm so sorry. I didn't mean for it to happen, but we just couldn't help ourselves."

"I'm sure you couldn't." She caught her books as they slid from his arms. "And of course you pleased your families. That's always of primary importance."

Though vastly relieved, she still felt a twinge of irritation that she had not been the one to speak up first.

"I'm so sorry," he said. "I can't tell you how sorry I am. I wouldn't have broken your dear heart for anything."

Becca leaned against the trunk of a nearby elm, her head lowered, her books clasped to her breast.

"Oh my dear girl." Winston reached out and touched her shoulder. "I *have* broken your heart. I could kill myself."

"It's not necessary to be that extreme, Winston." She looked up at him, her eyes sparkling with tears. But not for the reason he assumed. "I'm fine," she murmured. "Really I am."

"Oh, Becca, I just knew you'd be a good sport about this. You're such a brave, strong girl." He looked relieved. "Your life will go on, Becca dear. In time, you'll find someone else who will care for you."

It was all she could do to keep from laughing out loud, but it would hurt his feelings; why would she want to do that when he had given her such a great gift: her freedom without guilt?

She managed a downcast sigh. "I understand, Winston. We can't help who we fall in love with."

The Lord really does work in mysterious ways.

twenty

Dear Peter,

I write to you with my heart in my hand.

The last months have been an emotional and spiritual journey for me. Hopefully, I am a kinder, more compassionate person for it. All I can say, my dearest, is please forgive me for not seeing what was right before my eyes. In looking back, it seems impossible that I could have missed it.

Yet, would I have been in this place if you had confessed your love sooner? I honestly don't know. I don't know if I would have been ready.

Perhaps I needed to move away from you and Papa and Whispering Bluff to get a different perspective, view you from afar to draw you close, to see how near paradise I really was.

Simply, I needed to grow up.

I love you, Peter, more deeply, more dearly than I ever could have thought possible, more than mere words can express. I cherish you with every beat of my heart and every breath I draw.

It's been a long road home, my darling, but one worth taking. I truly believe I'm a better, stronger woman for the journey. All I ask is that you let me spend the rest of my life proving it.

Forgive me, my dearest, for any hurt I have caused you. Be generous and lay it on the ignorance of youth.

Your devoted,
Becca

∾

December 1, 1899

Dear Becca,

It wasn't easy loving you. You were more than a habit; you were my breath, my life. All my dreams were tied up in you. But when I left you on the bluff that night and walked down into the grove, I vowed I was going to move on.

It was hard. I can't say it wasn't. There were times when I wondered if it was even worth it to go on. Seems impossible, doesn't it? That's how low I was.

But the Lord gave me comfort, and Uncle Jacob and, finally, Jane. During these last dark months when I didn't hear from you, without fail, she was there.

Gradually she and I formed a bond. Not like I felt for you, Becca. I'll never have that again, but kinship, a sympathy for each other, if you will.

I believe that a life worth living is a life worth sharing, and so last week, four days before I received your letter, I asked her to marry me. And she said yes.

Life takes us on strange paths. I can only trust that the good Lord knows what He's doing.

Always your devoted and loving servant,
Peter

twenty-one

December 1899

Becca shivered and drew her coat closer.

In the distance, a shimmering horizon floated between the ominous afternoon clouds and the flat, foreboding plain. A chill wind whistled through the slatted sides and around the corners of the old train station, whipping up dirty drifts of snow.

The wheels of the departing train ground faster, spewing out hot sparks that glittered and fell dead on the gray wooden planks at her feet. Through the ephemeral swirl of smoke, she saw Peter standing at the far end of the platform, his legs apart, his hands thrust into the pockets of his jeans. The collar of his jacket was pulled up to his ears and his Stetson pulled low over his eyes.

Slowly, hesitantly, she moved toward him. She wondered how he would greet her. Not the way she had imagined. She held no hope for that.

But when she had almost reached him, he opened his arms and she walked into them, and he held her, close and warm— and she could almost believe things might be as they should.

"Oh, Peter—"

"Don't, Becca." His voice cracked. For an instant, his embrace tightened, and then he released her and thrust her gently away.

So that was how it was to be.

"I'll get your suitcase," he said.

She watched him stride to the baggage cart and heft down the heavy piece of luggage with the ease of the strong young farmer that he was.

She couldn't take her eyes off him. Even as he came closer and took her arm, guiding her down the rickety platform steps and to the waiting buggy.

"Uncle Jacob was disappointed not to be here, but his arthritis is acting up."

"Is it worse?" she asked, worried.

"About the same. It's the cold weather." He helped her up into the covered carriage and tucked a Pendleton blanket around her knees.

"Will Helga be there?" she asked as he hopped into the seat beside her and picked up the reins.

"She wouldn't miss welcoming you home." He snapped the reins. "The house smells like Christmas."

"I hope she left something for me to do." Becca smiled at him. "I may not be much of a cook, but I like to bake at Christmas."

"Nobody can beat your gingerbread men, that's for sure." He returned her smile.

"Not even Jane?" she murmured.

He glanced at her but didn't answer.

Why did I have to say that?

They continued in awkward silence for several minutes, sitting shoulder to shoulder in the small buggy, swaying against each other with each bump in the road.

Even though she didn't allow her gaze to wander and kept it straight ahead, she was achingly aware of everything about him, his sculpted profile beneath the lowered Stetson, his firm mouth, the flick of his dark lashes. She was aware of his gloved hands gripping the reins, and the press of his strong thigh against the volume of her skirt.

He turned his head. "Don't you notice something different?"

I've noticed only you.

She frowned. "Oh! Where's old Henry?" She turned, concerned. "You didn't have to put him down?"

"No, we just thought it was time to give him a rest, so we got this new filly."

"What's her name?"

"We thought you might have some ideas."

"Nell?"

He gave her a small smile. "You can do better than that. Don't disappoint me."

It wouldn't be the first time.

"Let me give it some thought."

They rode on, making small talk: the farm, how the new ranch hands were working out. . .the weather. . .always skirting the issue that quivered between them like a living thing.

"How's Jane?" Becca asked, finally.

"She's well."

"I'm glad."

"She's looking forward to seeing you."

"And I, her," Becca lied.

He knew she was lying.

She loved Jane. Who could help it? After Papa and Peter, she was always the first person Becca had wanted to see. Now she was the last.

Time would change that. It would have to. When Jane and Peter. . .

She couldn't think about it. Tears clouded her eyes. A recalcitrant one dribbled down her cheek, and she tried to brush it away without his noticing.

But he did. For an instant, his gaze softened then returned resolutely to the road.

Papa was waiting on the porch when they pulled up. Becca jumped from the carriage before Peter could help her down and ran up the steps into her father's arms. His cheek was warm.

At last she was home.

Helga stood in the doorway in her red dress that she always wore around the holidays and in her white apron, her face rosy from leaning over the kitchen stove.

"Get yourself out of the cold," she commanded in her throaty, no-nonsense voice. "There's hot cider. And I just pulled a punkin' pie from the oven."

They all crowded into the entry, Peter with her luggage,

Papa, Helga, and her, jostling and hugging.

Always she sensed where Peter stood—in the doorway, next to Papa, beside Helga—and then her eyes followed him up the stairs as he carried her suitcase to her bedroom.

Always in the next days, her eyes followed him and her palms would grow damp and her pulse pick up pace, and she would feel in her heart that ache, that longing that would not subside.

At odd, unexpected moments, she would find his gaze on her, and then they would each turn away, embarrassed.

Neither spoke of the letters or even acknowledged them. Why would they? Both had said what they needed to say. She wasn't sorry she had.

And so she went on, suffering that acute, exquisite pain of longing and loving.

"We waited to choose the tree until you arrived, Becca," her father said on the second morning she was there.

Peter stomped into the kitchen, his jacket buttoned to his chin, an ax in his gloved fist.

The gloves she had given him. Was that only a Christmas ago? He shoved his Stetson onto his head. "Come along, Becca."

They tramped across the yard, the ground crunching with each step, she in her fur-lined jacket, her cap pulled down over her ears. Snow powdered down on them as they trudged through the orchard toward the copse of evergreens on the edge of the Rikums' pond.

They hadn't even reached the wood when Becca stopped short. "That's the one I want!"

It wasn't five feet tall, had missing and broken branches, and those that remained were sparse of needles.

"That spindly little thing?" Peter made a face at her. "You must be kidding. Why, it's even more pathetic than the one we had last year."

"That's why I want it. It needs us, poor little tree. A strong breeze will blow it over. At least we can give meaning to its final days."

Peter grinned. "You're such a softy." And he began to chop.

Already the little evergreen had earned its keep by bringing him a smile.

They trimmed it that afternoon, a fire blazing on the grate, the whole house smelling of gingerbread and pine and spiced cider and popcorn, which they devoured. What they did not eat adorned the little tree with strings of cranberries and hanging walnut shells and cutout paper snowflakes and pinecones, until the spindly branches bent under the weight of its adornment.

The angel Papa had carved teetered at the top and around its base, the Nativity. Becca placed Mama's porcelain crèche just so on the mantel, exactly as it had always been. And for them all, at least for the moment, their hearts and home were filled with the merriment and joy of the Christmas season, and Becca forgot, almost forgot, what they were missing.

And then the phone rang.

Becca answered it.

"Hi, Becca, this is Jane."

Her reaction was immediate and visceral, and she hated herself for it. But she couldn't help it. "Hi, honey. Good to hear your voice."

If only it were true.

"Good to hear your voice, too. I can't wait to see you," Jane said.

"Me, too." Becca forced good cheer into her voice.

"That's not what I'm calling about. . .well, maybe in a way it is. We've had an accident of sorts here in town."

"Is anyone hurt? Where's Doc Warner?"

"Where he always is when we need him. Somewhere in Timbuktu. I'll sure be glad when you finish medical school. Everybody around here will be. Probably Doc Warner the most! Anyway. . ." Jane always seemed to be able to continue without taking a breath. "This young woman, *very, very, very* much with child, collapsed in the post office. She's a stranger. Just passing through, I suppose. She seems quite disoriented, and frankly, we—Daddy and I—don't quite know what to do with her. Of course I thought of you."

"Do you think she's about to deliver?"

"What do I know? That's your department. May I bring her over?"

"Of course. What I don't know, Helga does. We'll have the downstairs bedroom ready when you get here."

"I knew you'd take her. You're such a dear. I can't thank you enough; I'm going—"

"Hang up the phone, Jane, and get over here."

She heard a click. "By the way, Hazel, good evening. Say hello to Henrietta."

There was a "Harrumph" and another click, and Becca hung up the party line.

Jane arrived in a little over an hour in a very fancy buggy drawn by a prancing black gelding.

"My, my, what have we here?" her father murmured, standing on the porch next to Becca.

Peter hurried down the steps, and Jane reached out for his assistance. The smile she gave him radiated with the warmth of her feelings as she clung to his hand and looked into his eyes, and Becca witnessed for the first time the intimacy that they shared.

She wanted to turn and run back into the house.

Of course she couldn't, for her own pride's sake, for her sweet friend who was quite innocent, and for Peter—but especially for the frail young woman who Peter and Jane were helping from the buggy.

She looked so bedraggled that Becca was reminded of that spindly tree they'd just decorated, except that she came already adorned, and quite elegantly. Becca could see, even from a distance, that her red-velvet, fur-lined cape, with its hood falling in rich folds around her pretty face, was of the highest quality.

It didn't take a medical doctor in the making to tell that the woman was getting close to the moment of delivery, the way she walked, the way her face was pinched with pain.

Peter lifted her in his arms and followed Becca into the front hall and back to the bedroom next to the kitchen that the family had hurried to prepare.

As Peter laid the woman on the bed, Becca thought fleetingly that the last time they had used the room was when Mama lay dying.

But she had little time to ruminate on that with the challenge that lay ahead.

She shooed Peter and Papa from the room. After examining the young woman, she turned to Helga. "With my school learning and your having produced five children and practically being the town midwife, I think Mary Smith is in good hands!"

Jane refused to leave. Becca had a fleeting disappointment about that, but as always, her sweet friend put her hands and heart to good use.

Jane spent her time lining Helga's laundry basket with clean blankets to make a bassinet for the newborn. She found an old flannel sheet that she cut into squares and busied herself hemming them into new diapers.

And then she fixed dinner for the men.

At dawn, amid the flurry of activity universal at a birthing, the two napping men and Jane were aroused by a new baby girl who entered the world, squalling.

twenty-two

"She's a beauty, all right," Jacob said as he and Peter viewed the swaddled infant cradled in her mother's arms.

"Isn't she," Peter murmured, watching Becca who was sitting quietly in a chair beside the bed, gazing at the small bundle with such tenderness in her weary gray eyes it made his heart ache.

How he wanted to reach out and touch the wisps of disheveled ringlets that had escaped from her once tidy knot, to stroke her cheek, to hold those steady, capable hands that had such gentleness. He would have given anything to have the freedom to lift her in his arms and hold her close, and tell her how much he loved her and how proud he was of her.

So lost was he in his thoughts that he was startled to suddenly meet her lifted gaze.

Their eyes locked and held. A chord of understanding, deeper, more profound, more fraught with meaning than words could possibly express, passed between them.

She glanced away, as if scorched by the soul-searing pain of it.

Don't look away. Stay with me for just one moment more. See into my heart what I dare not say.

But she didn't.

Reluctantly he turned away. . .and found himself staring into Jane's wide, lavender eyes.

She stood in the bedroom doorway, backlit by the bright kitchen behind her.

She had seen the look that had passed between him and Becca.

She knew.

Despair tightened around his heart.

A montage of emotions played across Jane's sweet face: hurt, pain. . .heartbreaking sadness. Abruptly she turned and rushed from the room.

Becca jumped to her feet, but Peter brushed past her.

"Jane, wait."

Jane grabbed her cape as she ran through the front hall, out onto the porch, and down the steps, Peter in pursuit.

But she was fleet, her little feet racing, as if she were fleeing the truth.

"Jane, wait."

At the carriage, she whirled around, her eyes bright from the tears shimmering on their surface.

"I'm going home now, Peter. My work is finished here for today. Have Becca tell Mary that she need not worry about her buggy or her fine horse. Daddy and I will see they're well cared for 'til she needs them. And tell her I'll be back soon to see how she's getting along. And tell Becca she was wonderful and met all my expectations and I'm so proud of her, and thank Helga for a stellar job and your uncle Jacob for taking in this poor lost soul, although I knew he would, that's just like him, and. . .and. . ." She took a sobbing breath.

"Jane—"

She held up her hand. "Don't blame yourself, Peter. It wasn't your fault. I always knew where your heart lay. I just love—admired—you so much, and when Becca went off to be a doctor and seemed interested in that Winston fellow, I thought maybe I had a chance." She shrugged. "Let's face it, Peter, I set my curls for you."

She gave him a bright, false smile, even as tears began to wet her cheeks. "This is all a blessing, really. You're such an honorable man, you might very well have gone ahead with. . .with everything. In time, all three of us would have been miserable." She tossed her head. "And I, for one, deserve better. I deserve to have a man who loves me best, where I'm the first choice, not the consolation prize."

She pulled herself up into the buggy without waiting for his help and picked up the reins.

"Now don't you all feel sad for me. I'm very disappointed, very disappointed, indeed. But I'll get over it. Like Jesus said: 'If thou canst believe, all things are possible to him that believeth.' And I do believe that better things are in store for me, Peter. Not that you aren't the best, but you know what I mean. I do believe it, with all my heart."

She snapped the reins and guided the gelding around.

Peter watched as the buggy rolled down the drive and out onto the road and until it disappeared over the far side of the bluff.

He took a deep breath and let it out slowly. He felt as if it was the first breath he'd taken since Jane had started her monologue. He felt disoriented, confused. . .euphoric. *Euphoric!* It took a moment, but once his head cleared, that was the only word to describe it.

The only sad spot was Jane, brave, sweet little Janie. It didn't seem fair.

༜

Like a guilty voyeur, Becca had watched the conversation between Peter and Jane from the kitchen window. She knew it was wrong, and it served no purpose other than to add to her misery.

Finally, she willed herself to turn away.

Weary from fatigue and sadness, she dropped down into Mama's rocker, resting her head against its cushioned back. She gazed into the fire laid by Peter at dawn, watching the flames jump and crackle above the burning logs. The scent of pine and smoldering cedar blended with the lingering Christmas smells from the night before.

It didn't seem possible it was just last night that they'd trimmed the little tree, which stood quite proudly now, in all its finery.

Behind her, Peter said, "Jane left."

She felt his hand on her shoulder.

The most natural thing would have been to reach up and

cover it with hers.

She rejected the impulse.

"She said she'd take care of Mary's horse."

"That's good of her."

Peter knelt down in front of her. He took both her hands in his. His great, soft brown eyes gazed up at her with such raw emotion that she couldn't bear to look at him and turned her head. "Oh, Peter, we mustn't."

She felt his hand on her cheek, insistent yet gentle as he drew her face toward him.

"She said she didn't want to be anybody's consolation prize." His voice broke, and he shook his head sadly. "Can you imagine Jane being anyone's consolation prize?"

Becca could hardly breathe. "You mean. . ."

He nodded.

"She saw it in our eyes, didn't she?"

"She's always known, Becca." He gave her a small, mocking smile. "I told you, everybody's always known but you. But she thought when you and Win—"

Becca covered his lips with her fingertips. "I've only had one love. Like you said, I was just the only one who didn't know it." She gripped his hands. She didn't want to wake up and find he wasn't there.

Tears stung her lids and begin to dribble down her cheeks. "It's only because I'm tired. . . ," she murmured. But it wasn't just that. They were tears of relief, too. "And incredibly happy." She smiled at him and then confessed, "And sad for Jane. Who's to say I loved you more?"

"I just can't believe it." Peter shook his head. "I just can't believe that two such fine women would care so much for a simple farmer like me."

"My darling." She threw her arms around his neck. "A farmer you may be, but simple? Never!"

"Oh, Becca," he breathed, pulling her down into his lap and gathering her in his oh-so-strong arms. He pressed his lips against hers, at first ever so gently, and then with mounting fervor until all those years of pent-up passion spilled out into that kiss.

Until Becca felt weak and satiated. . .and loved.

&

A heavy snow kept them inside that Christmas Eve, wrapped in their own cocoon of joy.

Becca and Peter stood gazing into the remains of the midnight fire, still smoldering on the grate.

She put her arm around his waist. "Well, we've made one person happy."

"Only one?"

"Papa is ecstatic!"

"That's a relief." He grinned. "I was really worried."

"A blessed Christmas, darling," she said, dropping her head onto his shoulder.

"It is indeed." He wrapped his arms around her. "We even have our own Mary."

"And our own little baby. . .Nancy." She grinned and nuzzled his neck.

"Someday," he said, "there'll be little baby Becca and Peter and—"

"Don't count your babies before they're hatched," she admonished him. "And that won't start for at least two Christmases, when I've finished school. I know it seems like forever."

"An eternity." He gave her a sound kiss. "But not when you consider how long I've already waited for you, dulcet girl."

"Be patient, my darling," she said, snuggling close. "In time you'll know just how dulcet your girl can be."

There were ever so many reasons why they should wait to get married, the disconsolate Peter admitted. The most persuasive: For the next two years they would be spending so little time together, he here in Whispering Bluff, she at the university.

Of course, he was right, Becca agreed sadly. But it just didn't seem fair when they loved each other so much.

"Still, you'll be home summers and Christmas," he said, arguing with his own logic.

"Maybe I can even squeeze time at Easter," she said, seeing a glimmer of possibility.

"Lots of people are separated longer than we'll be," Peter said. "Men who come west to homestead and send for their families, sometimes even years later; soldiers, like the ones stationed in the Philippines at this very moment, they left wives behind." He flushed. "Captains of ships at sea are gone for months at a time from their families. Why, you and I would see each other much more often than any of those folks."

"Maybe we could get married when I come home in the summer," she offered hopefully.

"Good idea! The minute you step off the train."

"Well—"

But the levelheaded, rational, reasonable, wonderfully wise, frustratingly prudent, madly impetuous, wildly in love Peter had already taken her in his arms and was kissing her profoundly.

The exact date could be worked out later.

২◓

The following July, it seemed Becca had hardly set her foot on the station platform when the frenzy of activities commenced.

The wedding was just two weeks away.

To begin with, the flurry of wedding gown fittings!

Jane, transcending her own heartbreak, had insisted on making the gown her gift. Becca suspected that her sweet friend's disappointment had been diminished by the arrival of the new schoolmaster, a handsome, tragically widowed Easterner with a young, motherless son.

After much back-and-forth communication by post, Jane had designed a stylish summer gown in an ivory spotted silk with a lace-trimmed scoop neck and princess skirt and puffed sleeves to the elbow, trimmed in lace. A wide satin sash of a deeper ivory, which emphasized Becca's slender waist, was gathered into a large bow in back, its tails trailing to the lace-trimmed hem.

On the wedding day, Jane wove Becca a crown of ivy, entwined with daisies, to match the nosegay she would carry.

She was Becca's one attendant, as Jacob would be Peter's.

Becca waited in the ivy-framed doorway of the little church, clinging to her father's arm. Ivy festooned from pew to pew on either side of the middle aisle, caught with white satin bows. Baskets of ivy and white daisies flanked the altar, where Pastor David stood, beside him, handsome and strong, her beloved Peter.

The new mother, Mary Smith, had volunteered to sing. Her angelic voice soared through the little sanctuary, the notes of "Ave Maria," pure and clear and reverent.

Becca looked at her father. His expression was pensive as he met her gaze. She knew that he, as she, felt her mother's presence in the soft breeze that wafted around them, in the robin that chirped in the shading oak above them, and in the sun dappling the steps on which they stood.

Mama would always be with her, as would her father. . .as would Peter.

Her heart filled with gratitude to God for providing the wonder of all His blessings, most especially the enduring love of all those she held so dear.

Once, Peter had confided Mama's last words, "Take care of our Becca."

"Oh, Mama, he always has," she whispered softly, "and he always will."

A Letter To Our Readers

Dear Reader:

In order that we might better contribute to your reading enjoyment, we would appreciate your taking a few minutes to respond to the following questions. We welcome your comments and read each form and letter we receive. When completed, please return to the following:

Fiction Editor
Heartsong Presents
PO Box 719
Uhrichsville, Ohio 44683

1. Did you enjoy reading *The Long Road Home* by Rachel Druten?
   ❏ Very much! I would like to see more books by this author!
   ❏ Moderately. I would have enjoyed it more if

   _____

   _____

   _____

2. Are you a member of **Heartsong Presents**? ❏ Yes ❏ No
   If no, where did you purchase this book? _____

   _____

3. How would you rate, on a scale from 1 (poor) to 5 (superior), the cover design? _____

4. On a scale from 1 (poor) to 10 (superior), please rate the following elements.

_____ Heroine	_____ Plot
_____ Hero	_____ Inspirational theme
_____ Setting	_____ Secondary characters

5. These characters were special because? _____
_____
_____

6. How has this book inspired your life? _____
_____
_____

7. What settings would you like to see covered in future
   Heartsong Presents books? _____
_____
_____

8. What are some inspirational themes you would like to see
   treated in future books? _____
_____
_____

9. Would you be interested in reading other **Heartsong
   Presents** titles? ❏ Yes ❏ No

10. Please check your age range:
    ❏ Under 18   ❏ 18-24
    ❏ 25-34   ❏ 35-45
    ❏ 46-55   ❏ Over 55

Name _____
Occupation _____
Address _____
City, State, Zip _____

Heart♥ng

Any 12
Heartsong
Presents titles
for only
$27.00*

HISTORICAL ROMANCE IS CHEAPER BY THE DOZEN!

Buy any assortment of twelve *Heartsong Presents* titles and save 25% off of the already discounted price of $2.97 each!

*plus $3.00 shipping and handling per order and sales tax where applicable.
If outside the U.S. please call
740-922-7280 for shipping charges.

HEARTSONG PRESENTS TITLES AVAILABLE NOW:

___HP556 *Red Hills Stranger*, M. G. Chapman	___HP636 *Renegade Husband*, D. Mills
___HP559 *Banjo's New Song*, R. Dow	___HP639 *Love's Denial*, T. H. Murray
___HP560 *Heart Appearances*, P. Griffin	___HP640 *Taking a Chance*, K. E. Hake
___HP563 *Redeemed Hearts*, C. M. Hake	___HP643 *Escape to Sanctuary*, M. J. Conner
___HP567 *Summer Dream*, M. H. Flinkman	___HP644 *Making Amends*, J. L. Barton
___HP568 *Loveswept*, T. H. Murray	___HP647 *Remember Me*, K. Comeaux
___HP571 *Bayou Fever*, K. Y'Barbo	___HP648 *Last Chance*, C. M. Hake
___HP576 *Letters from the Enemy*, S. M. Warren	___HP651 *Against the Tide*, R. Druten
___HP579 *Grace*, L. Ford	___HP652 *A Love So Tender*, T. V. Batman
___HP580 *Land of Promise*, C. Cox	___HP655 *The Way Home*, M. Chapman
___HP583 *Ramshackle Rose*, C. M. Hake	___HP656 *Pirate's Prize*, L. N. Dooley
___HP584 *His Brother's Castoff*, L. N. Dooley	___HP659 *Bayou Beginnings*, K. M. Y'Barbo
___HP587 *Lilly's Dream*, P. Darty	___HP660 *Hearts Twice Met*, F. Chrisman
___HP588 *Torey's Prayer*, T. V. Bateman	___HP663 *Journeys*, T. H. Murray
___HP591 *Eliza*, M. Colvin	___HP664 *Chance Adventure*, K. E. Hake
___HP592 *Refining Fire*, C. Cox	___HP667 *Sagebrush Christmas*, B. L. Etchison
___HP599 *Double Deception*, L. Nelson Dooley	___HP668 *Duel Love*, B. Youree
___HP600 *The Restoration*, C. M. Hake	___HP671 *Sooner or Later*, V. McDonough
___HP603 *A Whale of a Marriage*, D. Hunt	___HP672 *Chance of a Lifetime*, K. E. Hake
___HP604 *Irene*, L. Ford	___HP675 *Bayou Secrets*, K. M. Y'Barbo
___HP607 *Protecting Amy*, S. P. Davis	___HP676 *Beside Still Waters*, T. V. Bateman
___HP608 *The Engagement*, K. Comeaux	___HP679 *Rose Kelly*, J. Spaeth
___HP611 *Faithful Traitor*, J. Stengl	___HP680 *Rebecca's Heart*, L. Harris
___HP612 *Michaela's Choice*, L. Harris	___HP683 *A Gentlemen's Kiss*, K. Comeaux
___HP615 *Gerda's Lawman*, L. N. Dooley	___HP684 *Copper Sunrise*, C. Cox
___HP616 *The Lady and the Cad*, T. H. Murray	___HP687 *The Ruse*, T. H. Murray
___HP619 *Everlasting Hope*, T. V. Bateman	___HP688 *A Handful of Flowers*, C. M. Hake
___HP620 *Basket of Secrets*, D. Hunt	___HP691 *Bayou Dreams*, K. M. Y'Barbo
___HP623 *A Place Called Home*, J. L. Barton	___HP692 *The Oregon Escort*, S. P. Davis
___HP624 *One Chance in a Million*, J. M. Hake	___HP695 *Into the Deep*, L. Bliss
___HP627 *He Loves Me, He Loves Me Not*,	___HP696 *Bridal Veil*, C. M. Hake
_____R. Druten	___HP699 *Bittersweet Remembrance*, G. Fields
___HP628 *Silent Heart*, B. Youree	___HP700 *Where the River Flows*, I. Brand
___HP631 *Second Chance*, T. V. Bateman	___HP703 *Moving the Mountain*, Y. Lehman
___HP632 *Road to Forgiveness*, C. Cox	___HP704 *No Buttons or Beaux*, C. M. Hake
___HP635 *Hogtied*, L. A. Coleman	___HP707 *Mariah's Hope*, M. J. Conner

(If ordering from this page, please remember to include it with the order form.)

Presents